ALPHA'S RESCUE

RENEE ROSE
LEE SAVINO

Copyright © June 2022 Alpha's Rescue by Renee Rose and Lee Savino

All rights reserved. This copy is intended for the original purchaser of this e-book ONLY. No part of this e-book may be reproduced, scanned, or distributed in any printed or electronic form without prior written permission from the author. Please do not participate in or encourage piracy of copyrighted materials in violation of the author's rights. Purchase only authorized editions.

Published in the United States of America

Midnight Romance, LLC

This e-book is a work of fiction. While reference might be made to actual historical events or existing locations, the names, characters, places and incidents are either the product of the author's imaginations or are used fictitiously, and any resemblance to actual persons, living or dead, business establishments, events, or locales is entirely coincidental.

This book contains descriptions of many BDSM and sexual practices, but this is a work of fiction and, as such, should not be used in any way as a guide. The author and publisher will not be responsible for any loss, harm, injury, or death resulting from use of the information contained within. In other words, don't try this at home, folks!

WANT FREE BOOKS?

Go to http://subscribepage.com/alphastemp to sign up for Renee Rose's newsletter and receive a free books. In addition to the free stories, you will also get special pricing, exclusive previews and news of new releases.

Download a free Lee Savino book from www.leesavino.com

1

Teddy

The sun warms my side of Bad Bear Mountain by the time I set out on the trail for my morning run. Something in the wind pulls me toward the summit.

Typically, I head past the town or towards the family cabin, but it's later in the day than usual, and I don't want to be accosted by my neighbors or any of my brothers. The town of Bad Bear has a population of only two hundred spread over the mountain, but some days, it feels like a fishbowl, and lately everyone's been beating a path to my door.

If I go this way, I can avoid seeing anyone and get some peace. That's what I tell myself, anyway, but the decision feels less rational than instinctual. My bear's guiding me.

Maybe there are early berries up on the peak.

I need a good hard run, and then maybe a long flight to take my mind off things. How long has it been since I've been in my bird? The helicopter taxi business has been slower than usual, but that's another thing I don't want to think about. I could contact the Black Wolf pack up in Taos to get jobs, but I keep putting it off.

Maybe my brothers are right, and I am becoming a hermit. But my bear has been riled up, more surly than usual, ever since our last mission. I took a break, even stopped doing flights up to Taos or visiting my wolf pack friends. I told myself I was giving them space, but the truth is, the sight of them happy with their mates brings up too much shit.

No matter how hard I run, I can't outpace the past.

The day is fine with a clear blue sky, but a gust of wind tells me we're getting a rain storm this afternoon. It's been a wet spring, and more flowers are blooming than usual. But the flash of bright pink ahead of me on the trail isn't a native flower blooming in the wild.

There. My bear wants me to charge forward. Instead, I stop running and slip into stealth mode, sidling up to a cluster of pines that can hide my bulk.

The pink color belongs to a floral scented human. Her dark skin is set off by bright pink. Even her water bottle is the same outrageous color. Who goes hiking dressed like that?

The wind shifts, and I catch her scent again. Flowers and honey, and something more. Most human women smell fussy with the fake scents of body lotion. But this human smells clean as rain, like creosote.

I stalk her a few paces before I realize what I'm doing. Usually, I stay away from humans, especially females. They're trouble, and I'd ban them from the mountain if I could. Which I can't. Our little town loves tourists, and no matter how much I protest, the mayor keeps coming up with schemes to lure more of them here.

Of course, if more of the tourists looked like this one, I wouldn't mind. After a few minutes of stalking, I'm close enough to get a clear view of her when she stops to drink some water. With her free hand, she flips her long braids– black with neon pink tips– behind her shoulder, then props her fist on her well-rounded hip. The move makes her breasts jiggle. There's some glorious cleavage packed into that eye-wateringly offensive outfit. I don't normally have anything against the color pink, but this shade is bright and blinding, as subtle as an ice pick to the eye.

I can't stop staring.

She moves along the trail, head high, braids swishing over her swaying backside.

I keep following quietly, keeping my distance. I'm barefoot, in old jeans that have more holes than denim and a shirt so threadbare it's almost see-through. My beard is reaching Biblical proportions. It's soft though.

I realize I'm rubbing my face and drop my hand. Why do I care what I look like? It's not like I'm heading to a date. I don't date. Not anymore.

Even if I did date, I wouldn't date a human again. I made that rule when I was eighteen and haven't broken it once since then. I haven't even been tempted to break it.

So why is the scent of this little human hitting so hard?

Overhead, a bird lands on a branch and chirps. Then it sees me and falls silent.

The little human whirls around. "Bentley? Is that you?"

I freeze, but like all werebears, I've been hunting and tracking since I could walk. What didn't come naturally, I learned in my special forces unit. There's a vale of pine trees, three laurel bushes, and a boulder between her and me. The distance and the sun dappled shadows camouflage me, and I'm standing downwind. Not that she can scent me. Humans never can.

"Bentley," she calls again. "I know you're there. You're not funny."

From the trail above, another human comes crashing through the brush. A male human, pasty pale and smelling sour.

"I'm right here. Jesus, Lana," he says. "I had to take a leak."

What an asshole. I hate the way he talks to her.

"Oh," her voice softens. "Just tell me next time. I thought you were a bear."

"I'd be so lucky," the guy mutters, and I have to stifle a growl.

"I heard that," she retorts, with more fondness than her rude companion warrants. If it were me, I'd bite his head off.

Maybe I still will.

The two continue huffing and puffing their way up the mountain, bickering like a couple on a sitcom. I follow, listening closely. I don't know why I don't just move on. They're two hikers. Nothing special. But my bear doesn't want me to lose sight of them.

"Mom and Dad would have loved this," she says. Her voice is smooth and musical as a dove's, while her companion whines like a circular saw.

So Lana and Bentley are not a couple—they're brother and sister. Stepsiblings.

He's munching on overpriced beef jerky and tosses the yellow wrapper on the side of the trail when he finishes his snack. The female whirls on him. "No. Absolutely not. We do not litter."

He mumbles something but picks it up and thrusts it in his pack. Next he goes to toss away a half eaten granola bar and she chides him again. "We're not supposed to leave human food, Bentley. Remember? Don't feed the bears."

"Yeah, yeah…" He waves a hand like he's swatting a fly.

Disappointment flashes over the woman's face, and I find myself a few feet closer to the hikers than I should be, half a second from introducing my fist to the asshole's face.

She flourishes a bright pink canteen. "Do you want some water?"

"No."

"Trail mix? I made it myself." She pulls out a bag filled with what looks like almond slivers and M&Ms. "Only the good stuff." She scoops a handful into her mouth and chomps. "Mmmm, so good. Come on, big bro, have a taste."

"Let's just get this over with. How far do we have to go?" He props his boot up on a rock and ties it, glowering at the white flowers blooming at his feet as if they're a pile of dog poop.

"All the way to the top."

"They won't know if we just dump their ashes off the side here." He gestures to a nearby ledge.

She props her hands on her hips. "We're supposed to be remembering them. This is a memorial hike. Just you and me." She swings a pink and black pack down and pulls out a fancy urn. The gold leaf painted in swirls along the side flashes in the spring sunlight. She holds it up. "Look, I know this is hard…"

The brother crosses his arms, a bored expression on his face. He looks as though he's waiting for his latte order, not grieving dead parents.

"…but it's what they wanted," she forges on. "They cared enough to stipulate this memorial hike in the will." She presses the urn to her chest. "They wanted us both here, to make memories."

The guy's mouth twists like he saw something distasteful. "The only reason I'm doing this is because it's a requirement in the will. As soon as we're done, you'll inherit your half of the money, and I'll inherit mine. Then we never have to speak again."

"Look, Bentley. I know we didn't get along as kids." She gives a forced laugh. "I know you're the one who ripped the heads off my Barbie dolls and stuck them on shish kebab skewers when I was six. I've forgiven you, by the way." She waits for him to respond, but he keeps on hiking.

"And I'm still sorry for telling mom and Roger you were the one who filled my favorite teddy bear with fireworks and set my bed on fire. I didn't know they would send us both to boarding school for the rest of our education."

Bentley acts like he didn't hear.

"I'd love to have a relationship with you now that we're adults. I thought we could use this hike to connect."

"Think again."

What a dick. I don't know why I care, though. Why am I even eavesdropping on this sad but irrelevant conversation? I should retreat, but my feet don't want to put distance between me and the female.

Which is crazy. She's human. Off limits.

Not mine.

My bear seems to disagree.

Which is why I hover just out of sight like a stalker, sipping down her scent.

No. I grit my teeth and force myself to slip away. The sooner I get distance between me and the sweetly-scented female, the better. Nothing good can come of hanging around a tempting human.

I learned that the hard way.

LANA

I can't shake the feeling that someone is watching.

After I've turned and scoured the woods for the *n*th time, I ask Bentley, "Did you hear that?"

"What?"

"There's something in the woods. I thought I saw…" I stop and shade my eyes. My memory tells me there was a shadow gliding between the trees a second ago, but now there's nothing there. "…Maybe it was just a bird."

"Maybe it's a bad bear going to come out of the woods and eat you."

I wrinkle my nose at him. "You sound like you're looking forward to that."

"Maybe I am."

I shake my head. I give up–I can't bridge the relationship between Bentley and me. Our parents would've wanted it–I think that's why they contrived this little memorial ritual for us–and I did my best to connect, but he's an ass. I have my standards.

I tromp on, rubbing away the prickling sensation at the back of my neck.

Bentley rounds on me and screws up his face like he smelled sweat-soaked wool socks. "And what the fuck are you wearing?" he asks like he's been criticizing me out loud all along.

"I'm so glad you asked." I strike a pose. "This is the all-new hiking line by GoddessWear."

Bentley sniffs and brushes past me, screwing the top back onto his water bottle. He doesn't even appreciate the high-tech fabric cut on a bias to lay flatteringly across my curves. I am a short queen and wonderfully round, and my new outfit is sporty and sexy at the same time. "No one makes cute hiking clothes in Goddess sizes," I tell Bentley. "So I set out to do something about it." I can't hide the immense pride in my voice.

"Did it have to be that color?"

"What's wrong with pink? It's my favorite color."

Bentley looks me up and down and sniffs. "It's so bright, they'll be able to see you from Santa Fe. Does it glow in the dark?"

"Yes," I say with triumph. "In case I get lost or fall in a ravine. Easier for the rescuers to find me."

He marches on, grumbling under his breath.

"Accidents happen," I trill and scramble after him.

"They sure do." I don't know why it sounds like Bentley's gloating. He pinches the bridge of his nose. "Why did my dad want to be tossed off this mountain anyway?"

I bite my lip before I bite his head off for referring to the spreading of our parents' ashes as *getting tossed off this mountain.*

I am made of sunshine. That's what my mom used to tell me, anyway. It was probably a learned coping mechanism for living with a stepbrother who hated me and being raised by nannies and very uninvolved rich parents.

My mom and my stepdad, Roger, weren't very present as parents. After boarding school, I moved out on my own.

I pause to rub my chest, but it's an automatic gesture, not a necessary one. The tight knots under my breastbone have eased. I did love my parents, but the shock and horror of the private plane crash that took their lives has worn off. I'm tired and a little bit empty, and I'm ready for this step in the grieving process. The urn with their ashes has been on my mantle in my house in Hollywood Hills for a year and a half.

"They had fond memories of visiting here," I say. "It

was the third stop on their honeymoon. After Park City and before Taos."

"I'm sure it was your mom's idea. Why anyone would willingly come to this shitty mountain is beyond me."

"What are you talking about? This mountain is perfect. It's like a postcard. Everything about it is so picturesque."

"Picturesque? What the fuck about this place is picturesque?" He wrinkles his nose like he's smelling dog poop.

"Everything," I rush to defend. "The pink mountains, the little town. Even the name is cute."

"Who names a mountain, *Bad Bear Mountain*?"

"The people who lived here, obviously. Maybe there's a bear problem." Oops, that probably would've been good to know before we went on an extended hike in the wilderness.

I try to search the internet for more info about Bad Bear Mountain and how it got its name, but the web page won't load.

We reach the summit around noon. I don't have to check my phone for the time— I can tell because the sun is directly above us. I'm practically a boy scout.

"Okay." I drop my poles and pack. Everything I've been carrying has gotten heavier in the past thirty minutes. "This is it. You want to do the honors, or shall I?"

Bentley makes an impatient gesture. "Get it over with."

"Not exactly the respect Mom and Roger deserve, but okay." I pull out the urn and head for a crop of rocks and a boulder that juts out over a scenic overlook.

While Bentley waits at the base, his arms crossed over his chest, I creep up the long ledge, planting each foot after the other with care. At the end of the rocky plank, I hold the urn close and peer over the edge. The long drop makes me dizzy. This high up, exposed, the wind whips my braids around my face.

"What are you waiting for?" Bentley calls.

"I'm waiting for the wind to blow the correct direction," I holler back. "I don't want to get a mouthful of Mom and Roger."

He grunts, conceding the point.

I stand at the edge of the world, hanging on to the urn. Now that I'm here, sweating in the hot sun, I wish I had done more to make this moment special. I should've prepared a speech. "Should I say a few words?"

"Lana, for fuck's sake," he shouts back.

Fine. I open the urn. "Goodbye Mom, Roger," I whisper to the wind and let the ashes stream away. I think about all the good times we had, the handful of winter break holidays and my graduation from boarding school. Our parents traveled a lot and lived their own lives, but the time we did share was special. And we certainly lacked for nothing. When I needed funds to start my company–

"Are you going to stay up there all day?"

"I'm saying goodbye," I shoot back over my shoulder. "They were our parents."

"No. That was *your* mom and *my* dad. We're not a family. We never were. And now it's over." His voice gains a sinister edge.

I press my lips together. I could ask him why he has to be so rude, but he's always been like this to me. Would it have killed him to be nice to me, his younger step sister? I'd always wanted a sibling. The smallest bit of kindness, and I would have adored him.

When I turn, Bentley is waiting at the bottom of the ledge. There's a look of ugly glee on his face, and something flashes in his hand, reflecting the bright sunlight.

A knife.

"Bentley?" I stare at the weapon. "What are you doing?"

"You're so stupid," he spits. "You think I'm going to tromp up all the way here and miss this opportunity? They'll think you died in an accident. And I'll mourn you. Hell, I can put you in that urn." He jerks his chin towards the now empty urn, and I clutch it to my chest as if it can protect me.

"What are you talking about?"

"Do I have to spell it out?"

"Seriously, Bentley, what the heck? Put that down. Someone could get hurt."

"That's the plan." Bentley's forehead is red and shiny. He's sweating so furiously, his grip on the knife must be slippery.

I take a step back.

"Yes, that's it," he motions with the knife. "Move back."

A few pebbles tumble out from under my shoe and bounce down the ledge, disappearing from view. "But...I'll go over the edge."

"Exactly." His grin is evil.

"This is ridiculous." I put my hands on my hips. "Why would you want to kill me? Is this about the money? The inheritance? We're both getting equal shares of the estate. The will splits the assets down the middle. The houses, the investments–"

"It should've been all mine!" Spit flies from Bentley's mouth. "It was my dad's fortune!" Sweat sluices over his threadbare eyebrows and pours into his eyes. He goes to mop his brow with the hand that is holding the knife.

"Ooh, careful." My hand flies out to warn him from slicing up his own head. "Don't hold the knife like that. You'll cut yourself."

Bentley lowers the knife and wipes his head with his free hand.

Am I really talking him through how to properly hold a knife while he's trying murder me? I should be trying to get away.

I scuttle to the side of the big, jutting rock, but my options are limited. The side of the ledge is steep, and if I put a foot wrong, I'll fall. Best case, I'll fall a few feet to the boulders below. Worse case…

"Just a little further." Bentley creeps up the ledge towards me.

I glance behind me at the five hundred foot–or more–drop. "No." I plant my feet. "You're not going to make me toss myself over the edge. You'll have to knife me."

"So be it." He takes another step forward, and despite myself, I scoot an inch back.

"So that's your plan? You're just going to knife me? How is that going to look like an accident?"

"I'll push you over the edge. Maybe I'll just leave your body, and no one will find you." He sounds uncertain.

"What if I'm not dead?" I cross my arms over my chest, then rethink the position and put my arms out for balance, taking frequent, dizzying glances down at the five hundred foot fall. "What if I just break all my arms and legs?"

"Oh, you'll die," he says. "I'll make sure of it."

"You're going to climb down and bash my head in?" I don't know what's more offensive. That he's trying to murder me, or that he's doing it badly.

Bentley's face is getting redder by the second. "This is just like you," he grits out. "Why do you have to be so difficult?"

"That's not fair," I shoot back. "I've been nothing but accommodating."

"I'm not giving up half of my inheritance. It was my Dad's money to start with. You and your mom were just riding his coattails. Besides, both our parents knew you were the stupid one—"

"If I'm so stupid, why are you the one who's doing such a bad job of trying to kill me? Why am I a CEO?" I shout over the wind. The gust tugs on my braids, and more pebbles roll over the edge. A strong enough gust, and I'll topple over with them.

It's now or never.

I'm going to have to throw myself toward Bentley and see if I can rush past him. Then I'm going to have to outrun him all the way to the rental car.

God, I hate running. I do not have a body that is built to run. I have a body that was built to lounge beautifully on a divan. And to swim. I love to swim.

I fake left, then dash right, but Bentley blocks me. The knife is between us, pointy side up. Not good.

Other than the unnatural flush staining his cheeks, Bentley's face is horribly pale. His eyes are wide and staring, the whites flashing as if he's more frightened than I am. Is that why he was anxious and sweaty this whole hike? He was plotting to kill me?

I make a break for it, and when Bentley thrusts, I smash his knife hand with the urn. He yelps and drops the weapon but grabs me with his free hand. We both grapple with each other—him trying to haul me off balance, me trying to push him away.

He really is going to push me over the edge. I let my body grow heavy and fall to the ground, dragging him with me. Except now I'm lying in shards of the urn. And Bentley's closer to the knife.

Moving more quickly than I thought possible, he snatches up the wicked-looking weapon and brandishes it.

I put up a hand as if my empty palm can stop him, and try to scramble to my feet, but it's too late. He's almost on me—

A roar blasts over us, and a dark shape crashes out of the trees. The ground shakes, and I lose my balance. For a few awful seconds, I teeter on the edge.

I throw myself forward, careening down the ledge towards safety. Toward Bentley and the knife. I nearly became a pink smear at the base of a scenic overlook, but that's the least of my problems.

A freaking monster just ran out of the woods. Brown fur, black snout, long teeth. All my wildlife expertise comes from watching animal videos on Tiktok, but I know a bear when I see one. A bad bear.

He's freaking huge, big as a car. Not a little car, either. An SUV. The ground thunders under his paws as he races toward us. His open mouth is bigger than my head, ready to eat me and Bentley in one bite.

Now would be a good time to remember what to do when faced with an attacking bear. Run? Play dead? Scream my head off and hope someone comes to help?

Bentley is already doing that—his scream high and shrill and loud as a chorus of teenage girls at a K-pop concert, tinged with terror instead of adoration. He drops the knife. It bounces off the boulder and wedges between two rocks. In his haste to escape, he shoves me, and I fall. Not all the way down—just a few feet. The world tilts, the trees and sky spin around me. My forehead smashes into something and light bursts behind my eyes.

When the light fades, I'm on my back, staring up at the sky. A cluster of rocks broke my fall.

At least Bentley's stopped screaming. Either he's gone, or the bear ate him.

I blink in the silence. There's something wet dripping

ALPHA'S RESCUE

to my face. Maybe Bentley will get my half of the inheritance after all.

I grit my teeth, willing myself to live, if only to spite Bentley, when a huge shadow falls over me. It's the bear, looming over me, his shaggy face close to mine. I had a teddy bear as a child. The real life version is nothing like it. Except the ears–those are round, fuzzy and super cute.

The bear grunts. His hot breath hits my face.

This is the end. I can't talk my way out of this one.

I could try to get up and run, but these rocks under my back are weirdly comfortable. I let my head fall back with a clunk. Pain knifes through my head, and a black blanket drops over my face, blotting out the world.

Teddy

Thank fuck my bear drew me back to the pink-clad female. I arrived at the summit just in time to see the pasty male threaten her with a knife.

I didn't think. I didn't wait. I just shifted. And attacked.

Now her attacker's gone, and she's lying in a pink pile on the rocks with blood dripping down her face.

I would chase him, but I don't want to leave her.

Still in bear form, I sniff her hair. Blood. She hit her head when her stepbrother pushed her. Now she blinks up at me, her gaze unfocused.

I'm probably freaking her out right now.

Before I can stop it, the shift comes over me. I tense and try to fight it, but it's like trying to stop sneezing midsneeze. My spine arches and cracks, and my form flows from the giant bear shape back to human. I stagger on two feet, chest heaving.

What the fuck was that? My bear just forced me to

turn. In front of a human. I've never been out of control like that.

I stretch out a hand, flicking my fingers to get rid of the cramps. I'm still standing over the little human, and even though my shape is smaller, I still tower over her.

Shit. Did she see me turn?

Her eyelids flutter. I hold my breath, but her eyes stay closed. But they were open before, right? Which means she knows my secret.

This is a mess, and I just made it worse.

She seems unconscious now. If she wasn't lying on a pile of rocks with a trail of red running from her temple to chin, she'd look like she just lay down for a nap.

I touch her hand, and it's limp. She's out, probably with a head injury. Humans are so fucking fragile. She needs medical help. It might not be a great idea to move her now, but I can't leave her, in case her psycho stepbrother comes back and finishes what he tried to start.

I need to get her out of here.

After checking her open wound, which bled a lot but seems to be clotting now, I carefully scoop her into my arms. Lifting her takes no strength. She's a pleasant, warm armful, and as I try to steady her head, she mumbles something and snuggles closer. Her honeyed scent tickles my nose.

I move as quietly as I can. I'm naked, the remains of my clothes shredded by the treeline. If she wakes now, I'll have a lot of explaining to do.

I'll get her somewhere safe, get her checked out, and deal with her questions then. I'll have a few questions of my own. Starting and ending with whether or not she saw me turn from a big bear into a human.

The knife is still in the rocks, glinting up at us. I'll send one of my brothers to get it and her bright pink pack. Now that she's in my arms, I don't want to risk jostling her.

I'm striding towards tree cover when her head tilts back and her beautiful brown eyes fix onto my face. Damn, she woke up fast. She still looks a little dazed. Her eyebrows tighten to a V, then smooth out. I turn into a statue as her small hand comes up and touches my cheek.

"Bear," she mouths. She molds her fingers over my face, and repeats intently, "bear," before her hand falls. Her eyes close, and her head sags onto my shoulder once more.

Shit.

2

Teddy

The lovely human remains mostly unconscious all the way to my cabin. When I set her on my bed, she immediately curls up into a ball. I cover her with a blanket and draw the curtains to keep the room dark and cool. The sight of her in my bed is more than satisfying. I try not to think too hard about that.

I step out and make one phone call and spend a good fifteen minutes pacing my perimeter, checking for weak spots and sniffing the wind. I still can't believe I shifted right in front of her. Hiding the secret of our animals is the first thing we learn as shifters. Out of control shifting isn't just a rookie move, it's a deadly one. My younger brothers had some trouble with control when they were teens. Ma had to homeschool them until they could hide their animal properly. But at their worst, they wouldn't make such a fatal mistake.

What were you thinking? I chastise my bear, but he doesn't answer. I sense his satisfaction. He likes the little human, and now she's right where he wants her.

In my bed.

Shit, what a mess.

My brother finds me pacing in front of my cabin. I whirl as soon as I sense his silent approach. "Matthias."

My brother is dressed in his usual button down shirt and nice slacks. Unlike the rest of us, he actually holds a job around humans. I was lucky I caught him between appointments.

"Teddy." Matthias greets me with a nod that makes his glasses glint. He doesn't need glasses because he has perfect shifter vision, but he wears them anyway. "You okay?"

No, I stalked a female through the woods and rescued her from her murderous brother. Then I transformed right in front of her, like a fool. My bear might be completely out of control.

"Yep, just fine. Come in." I hold the door for him. We both have to duck our heads to enter the cabin, and when Matthias stands up straight in my living room, his tight black curls brush the exposed pine beams. He has a slimmer build, but he's a hair taller than me.

"Thanks for coming so fast," I say. "Did you go to the summit?"

"I found this." Matthias lifts the bright pink pack. "Along with broken pieces of pottery. But no knife."

"Shit." I scrub a hand over my face. I should've taken care of the knife right away, so her stepbrother couldn't come back for it. The female has me making all sorts of mistakes. "Did you see anyone?"

"No. Caught the scent of a couple of humans. One of them was her. The other is male."

"Her stepbrother. He tried to stab her, and when I surprised him, he ran." I'm itching to go out and find him, but until I know the female will be all right, I'm tethered to her side.

Matthias gives a calm nod as if I described something

normal. He's used to me giving him the barest details of my missions. Nothing fazes him. Plus, he's a doctor with human training, which made him the perfect brother to call to solve this dilemma. "Where's the patient?"

"In there." I point to my bedroom.

Matthias' eyebrows bounce. My cabin is small and cozy, with a one room kitchen and living room in front of the fireplace, and a small bedroom barely big enough to fit one wardrobe and my bed. "I could've put her on the couch, but people with head injuries need quiet and privacy, right?"

"Sure," Matthias says.

I don't add that the couch is too exposed. Too near the door. I need to keep her safe. I especially don't add the fact that the need to have her in my bed overrode all else.

I won't examine that urge too closely.

I take the human's pink bag, and Matthias unslings his black leather doctor's bag from his shoulder.

"I'll just go check on her now." He ducks in the bedroom, and I fight the urge to growl and follow him. I don't want anyone near the human female but me.

Mathias washes up in my bathroom before heading to the patient. When the bathroom door creaks, I can't fight my instincts any longer. I give up and hover in the door to my bedroom, watching Matthias lean over the bed to examine the female. He wears gloves, and his hands are gentle, but her brow creases as he touches her head.

"That wound looks nasty, but it's the least of our worries," Matthias says. "She probably has a severe concussion."

"Is that bad?" Human injuries make me nervous. Some of them die from bee stings or eating a peanut. How in the hell do I keep this one alive?

"Did you see how she hit her head?"

I lean against the doorframe, fighting the urge to rush past Matthias and gather the little human in my arms. "I was out for a run. She was hiking when her stepbrother tried to kill her. I stepped in, but in the commotion, she fell on some rocks."

Matthias accepts this with a nod. He's holding a small flashlight and shining the light into Lana's eyes. "How long has she been out?"

As I explain the details of the rescue, I squeeze into my bedroom and hover over Matthias. The female's scent fills the space, and my instincts are telling me to scoop up the little human and throw my brother out. Which is nuts. There's no reason for me to be so possessive over a human I haven't met.

"And you brought her here instead of to the hospital?" Matthias asks.

"She can't leave," I blurt without thinking. "Her stepbrother tried to kill her, remember?"

"You think he's still out there, searching for her?"

"He looked pretty determined."

"You going to go look for him?"

"She's the priority. Any idea why she's still unconscious?"

"The concussion. She did come to for a few minutes, correct?"

"Just under a minute."

Matthias grunts. He fiddles around in his bag and holds up a vial of dark green liquid. "Hold her head."

I shift around him to steady the patient. Her head looks so small between my huge hands. She really is a knockout—smooth, dark skin, sculpted cheekbones, cute little nose, plush lips.

Matthias sets the vial to her mouth and pours the

contents in. It smells weird, a metallic and herbal combination.

I stiffen. "What's that?"

"Just a little something I cooked up," Matthias murmurs, tilting the vial so it empties completely. "Come on, swallow. That's it."

"What's in it?"

"You don't want to know."

My growl surprises us both.

"It's a healing serum," Matthias says. "One of my concoctions. It'll help her head."

All my trepidation vanishes. Matthias is trying to help. "It's not a good sign that she's asleep this long, is it?"

"Not at all. But that should heal the worst." He tucks the empty vial back in his bag and pulls out a pack of gauze. "It'll take a moment to work. In the meantime, I can clean this cut. It doesn't look like there are any other contusions." He sprays a solution on the gauze and starts dabbing her head. "You need to keep her under observation for at least twenty-four hours. No more moving her or loud noises, if you can help it. She needs rest." He peers over the tops of his fake eyeglasses at me. "Can you take time out of your busy schedule to do that?" His voice is mild, not a hint of sarcasm as he says *busy schedule*, but I bristle as if it's a reproof.

The last time we spoke, he accused me of turning into a hermit. Of all my brothers, Matthias is the calm, quiet, thoughtful one. He's also the one who is most likely to resort to sarcasm and subtle ways of letting me know he's displeased. My other brothers would swing a fist in my direction. We Bad Bear brothers tend to use physical scuffles to sort things out, much to our Ma's chagrin.

"Yeah, I can manage that," I say.

"You can check her bag for a driver's license to learn her name."

"Lana. It's Lana."

Matthias raises a brow, and I scramble to explain. "I may have overheard her and her stepbrother talking earlier on the hike. I was out for a run when they passed by, and you know humans. They're loud." I let my voice trail off. The more I try to convince Matthias I wasn't stalking Lana, the less he's convinced. Maybe I shouldn't have called him. He's the least likely to annoy me, but he's also smarter than me and half my brothers combined. I can't fool him.

Matthias cleans up the human's head wound and bandages it. The whole time the patient is out, her chest rising and falling softly. When he finishes, he checks her pupils again. "Much better."

"Should she still be sleeping?"

"She's going to be fine. At this point, the sleep is healing. Now, when she wakes up, she might be disoriented. She's in a new place. And she never saw you, correct?"

I hesitate. There's more to the story I need to tell him, but not here. "I think so, but I'm not sure."

Matthias tosses the bloody gauze and trash into a small waste bag and removes his gloves.

"Wait, that's it?" I look from the sleeping patient to my calm brother. "You're done?"

"I've done all I can. The wound is clean, and it doesn't need stitches. She doesn't have a fever, and her pupils look fine now. No brain bleed."

Brain bleed? "Maybe we should get her to a hospital." I could lie, say I'm her husband. Stay close and guard her.

"Only if you want to get her out of your hair. The hospital can't do more than I've done. In fact, they would've done far less."

"What about…I dunno… tests?"

"An MRI and CT won't tell us if she has a concussion. We'll have to watch her symptoms and how she acts. Keep tabs on any behavior changes."

"How will I know her behavior changes? I don't know her."

"You can ask her when she wakes up." Matthias takes off his glasses and polishes them. I swear he only wears the fake glasses so he can use them like a prop in a play. Maybe it makes it easier to pretend to be human. With his glasses and outfit, he looks like a mild-mannered country doctor. It's a good disguise. "You have time to sit and watch her? Do you have any flights?" He's referring to my helicopter business. I do tours and chauffeur businessmen from Albuquerque to Taos in addition to working more dangerous jobs with my special forces buddies in the Black Wolf pack.

"No jobs. Business is slow."

"Hmmm." Matthias says nothing more, but his gaze is incisive, dissecting me. He knows I'm not telling him something.

I've got to fess up. "There's more. Another… complication."

Matthias stiffens. "Have you noticed any more bleeding?"

"It's not that." I signal him to leave the cabin. He washes up in the kitchen, packs his bag and exits quietly ahead of me. I take a deep breath of pollen-scented air as we walk out into the spring day. The meadow in front of my house is in bloom. Bees browse over the white and pink flowers my younger brothers planted for them, against my wishes. The female's honeyed scent follows me out here. It's so sweet the bees will be trying to get into the house soon.

Fuck. What have I done? It doesn't feel like my whole world has tilted on its axis, but it has.

Once we're to the edge of my wildflower-filled yard in view of the beehives through the trees, I stop and face my brother. Matthias and I are only a few months apart. Ma adopted us both around the same time. I'm closer to him than any of my other brothers, even my twin.

I still don't want to admit my fuck up to him. "I made a mistake." Damn, it's hard to get the words out. "She was unconscious and…I panicked. One second, I was in bear form, and the next…I couldn't stop the change. And…I think she saw me turn."

Matthias adjusts his glasses. I've studied interrogation techniques, so I know what he's doing, but after a minute of Matthias' silence, I crack and explain.

"My bear just forced me to turn. In front of a human. I've never been out of control like that."

Matthias' expression is thoughtful—not judgmental. "Has it happened before?"

"No, never."

"Maybe it'll be all right."

"If she saw me…"

"Then we deal with it. There's a protocol."

"Yeah." Protocol means marching the human to a vampire and holding her down while the leech hypnotizes her into forgetting our secret. "I was hoping to avoid that."

"It might be necessary." In light of this serious subject, Matthias' calm tone sounds cold. I stare at my reflection in his fake glasses. He acts so kind and gentle, I forget how ruthless he can be. He was the one who stood by my side when I had to deal with this situation before. He knows the depths of my pain and shame.

And now we're traveling down the same road. Still, I have to ask. Something makes me protective of the little human sleeping in my bed. "Getting mindwiped after a head injury… won't it mess her up?"

"It's not ideal. I can't promise it won't result in memory and cognitive problems." He sounds so clinical. What he's really saying is the cost of preserving our secret might ruin this human's life. This is the real Matthias, and the Mr. Rogers' cardigans and gentle bedside manner are all part of an act. The kindly doctor meant to lull humans into a sense of security as false as his glasses. He'll do what it takes to ensure our family survives. So will I. If the honey-scented human in my bed is collateral damage, so be it. It's a choice I've had to make before.

Family first.

"I don't know if she saw me change back to human. I don't know if she saw me changing into a bear in the first place. I guess I'll find out soon enough when she wakes." If she saw everything, she'll run screaming to the nearest newsroom. Just like Tiffany did.

"If you don't know if she saw anything, you'll have to keep her here until you're sure."

I grunt assent.

"Or you could take her to the nearest leech and get her mindwiped now. Preemptively."

"No," I snap.

"You want to get to know her before you mindwipe her?" Matthias asks, but it's a loaded question. My answer will tell him more than I want him to know.

Instead of answering, I glare at him.

"Or you can wait and see. It might not come to that." Matthias shoulders his black leather bag. "Call me the minute she wakes up, and I'll come back to do a proper exam."

"You can't stay?" As much as I want Matthias gone, it's

good for him to be close, in case the human starts convulsing or something.

"I have a house call scheduled."

"Who?"

There's a ghost of a smile lurking in the corner of Matthias' mouth. "Daisy."

I snort. "Daisy's healthy as a horse. She hasn't had so much as a cold in twenty years."

"She's eighty-nine. She says she wants to live to her 150th birthday."

"Good luck with that."

"Thanks, I'll need it. Other than a bite from a vampire, I have no way of granting long life to anyone."

"If anyone can live that long, it would be Daisy. But don't tell her about vampires. She might get ideas."

"Fates, no. Have you heard about her new idea to promote tourism?"

I groan. "Not bear rides."

"No, that was nonsense. She was never serious about that or the man-versus-bear hot dog eating contest. This is a new scheme."

I rub both hands over my face. "I don't want to know."

"She doesn't think up these things as a way of annoying you. She's trying to save the mountain. Speaking of which, I heard from Darius. He wants to—"

I know what he's going to say. "No."

"You don't even know what he requested." Matthias straightens his glasses, and I clench my fist to keep from smacking them off his face.

"I know I don't want to hear it."

Matthias says nothing, but I know he disapproves.

"Look." I wave a hand at my cabin. "Don't I have enough on my plate?"

"Fine. I'll stall him. See to your patient. When she

wakes up, if her head hurts, you can give her something. A mild painkiller, not aspirin." He pulls out a packet of Tylenol from his doctor's bag and hands it to me. "It'll help to put something cold against the injury. A bag of frozen peas will work."

"What about frozen blueberries?"

He nods solemnly as if I didn't say something stupid. "Blueberries are fine."

"I'll monitor her," I promise. "Thanks for coming."

"I'll be back after my appointments." He half turns to leave.

"Another thing," I catch his arm. "Don't tell anyone she's here."

"I won't, but you know that won't stop your visitors from finding out." Matthias nods to the beehives. "This time of year, Everest likes to check the bees."

I stifle a groan. Everest is my most enigmatic brother. "I don't know why he put the hives over here. He's got his own place."

"It's Everest. We don't know if he has his own place. He might just have a cave in the woods. I'm pretty sure he spends most of his time as a bear. Also, the Terrible Threes are looking for you."

My groan comes out a half growl, and Matthias can't stop his smile. "For fuck's sake, what do they want?"

"You'll have to ask them."

"No," I say. "Tell them I'm on a mission or something."

"They know where you live."

Shit. He's right. My house is Grand Central Station when my brothers want something. "Maybe I can move her…"

"Don't move her."

I go cold. "Did I do the wrong thing moving her before?" I wanted to get the lovely human to safety, but if I harmed her, I won't be able to forgive myself. "Do you think I made it worse?"

Matthias stares at me, unblinking. There's no hiding the concern in my voice, and now he knows more about my feelings for my unwanted guest than I do. I stiffen my back, so I don't twitch under his incisive gaze. "She'll be fine. The healing serum is fixing the serious injuries."

"But she's still sleeping—"

"Sleep is good. She won't heal as fast as we do, but the serum is helping. The more rest and relaxation, the better. When she wakes up, tell her to take a little vacation. Maybe she can rent your cabin." He's teasing me.

I scowl. "That's all I need. A paying tourist."

"Daisy will be pleased."

"Great. I live to please Daisy."

"One more thing, brother." Matthias tilts his head as if he just had a thought. His smile is gone, but I can hear it in his voice. "I don't know if you've realized, but the human…"

I brace myself for the parting shot. "What?"

"She's just your type." Before I can growl at him to get gone, Matthias ducks his head under a pine bough and strides away through the trees.

LANA

Light touches my face like a warm hand, and I wince. My head throbs. I move my face a little to the right and blink until the wall and window in front of me come into focus. The window is framed by the cutest curtains I've ever seen. The fabric is dark green with a parade of little brown bears trotting across them in even rows.

I blink and start to sit up, but the searing pain in my

head keeps me from moving far. I'm in a soft bed with worn plaid sheets and a forest green comforter. The walls are built of honey-brown Lincoln logs. The room is small, dominated by the four poster bed and a pine wardrobe in the corner to my left. To my right is a bedside table, also made of pine. On the tiny table is a lamp. Its shade is made of the same fabric as the curtains–green with marching brown bears.

Where am I? What happened? I reach for my memories, and there's a blank space and more head pain, so I give up trying to remember. I don't know how I got into this cabin, but someone who picks out cute curtains and a matching lampshade can't be a serial killer. Right?

I try again, and I'm able to sit up slowly and lean against the rough hewn pine headboard to take inventory once the room stops spinning. I'm still in my hiking outfit. It's a little dusty but otherwise holds no clues as to what happened to me. There's a bandage taped to my head. Panic makes me want to run to the nearest mirror to take a look, but my skull threatens to split if I try to swing my feet over the edge of the bed, so I sag back into the pillows instead.

My braids have a few pine needles in them. I brush these off onto the shaggy brown rug covering the rough pine floor. All this pine and plaid tells me I'm in a mountain cabin. And that fits. I'm on Bad Bear mountain.

It comes back to me slowly: my parents urn, my brother Bentley. Where is Bentley? We were going to hike up to throw the ashes off and fulfill our parents' wishes. The last thing I remember is us getting out of our rental car. When I try to remember past that, pain flashes through my head, bad enough to make my eyes water.

At some point, I hit my head, and someone bandaged it.

Bentley? Or the owner of this cute cabin? The room feels kinda homey for a rental. There are two closed doors, one at the foot of the bed, one and one to the left, opposite the single window and next to the big pine wardrobe. The wardrobe's door hangs open, revealing a row of big plaid shirts hung on one side and a few neat piles of folded clothes on the shelves. Unless mountain cabin rentals now come with complimentary plaid shirts, this is someone's home.

I can't do any more sleuthing until I can move, but there are worse places to recover. This room is inspiring me to design a new Christmas line for my company, Goddess-Wear™. The theme will be mountain chic. I'm thinking plaid pajamas, cozy nightgowns, and fluffy slippers. Cute little brown bears are definitely going to be making an appearance.

The big rough-hewn door in front of me creaks open, and in walks the most stunning man I've ever seen. He's a giant-sized Viking with buzzed blond hair and a beard raging out of control. His worn t-shirt is stretched over swollen pecs, and his biceps look like they're about to burst out of the sleeves. One deep flex of those bulging muscles, and his shirt will give up and fall to the floor, leaving him topless. And that would be a tragedy.

Not.

I'd get to examine the deep tan of his skin and the beautiful colors of his full sleeve tattoos. The ink above his elbow depicts a honey bee and a big brown bear.

Again with the bears. I love it when people stick to a theme.

"You're awake," the Viking rasps. His blond brows form a surly line. He looks grumpy. But I've dealt with grumpy ever since my mom fell in love with a big Hollywood executive type, moved us to Hollywood Hills, and stuck me with a cruel stepbrother. I meet grouchy with sunshine every time.

"Hey." I give a little wave and flinch when the movement jostles my head.

The Viking prowls into the room, his movements fluid for a man of his size. He crouches next to the bed, which puts his head even with mine. His grey eyes pierce me. "How you feeling, babygirl?"

Babygirl? Um, wow. Okay. That's cool. I don't know this guy, but he can call me babygirl anytime. And I do mean anytime.

He is every shade of big, brawny and beautiful. His sheer masculinity has my ovaries dropping eggs faster than a slot machine that just hit jackpot. I literally hear the bells going off–

No, wait. That's my headache. My hand rises to touch my forehead.

"Careful," he cautions, catching my wrist and turning over my hand. I have a few pieces of gravel still stuck to my palm. He brushes these off with gentle fingers.

Heat shoots through my body. *Oh my.*

"Are we acquainted?" My tone is a little too hopeful. Maybe Bentley and I finished the memorial ritual, and he left me to it, and I wandered into the little town of Bad Bear, had a cocktail at the olde-timey-looking bar, and met this Viking. Maybe he wooed me with descriptions of his cute curtains, and I accepted his invitation to get an intimate look at his bedroom.

And now it's the morning after. But if we had dirty, passionate sex, how did I get my head injury? My body wouldn't be sore like I fell off a cliff, it would be sore in a different, more delicious way. So maybe we haven't done it. *Yet.*

"What do you remember?" He searches my eyes carefully.

"Um. I came here and–ugh." A flash of pain streaks from temple to temple.

"Easy." His tone is gentle even though he looks annoyed. With his wild beard and intense stare, he has Resting Badass face. I'm finding it hard to catch my breath.

Or maybe it's his delicious scent and the proximity of all those muscles ready to burst out of the overworked fabric of his t-shirt. It's been a while since I've been on a date. I haven't had much time. After my parent's death, I threw myself into my business and brand. And now, I have no defenses against hot guys.

That's it. I'm just overwhelmed by all the muscly handsomeness of this modern day mountain Viking.

He's searching my face with those beautiful eyes of his.

"How did I get here?" I ask.

"You took a fall up on the mountain, and I carried you. What do you remember?" he repeats. It feels a little like interrogation.

"My head hurts," I mumble, which is the truth.

Abruptly he stands. I flinch backward at the sudden movement and his sheer size, and he rests his big hand on my shoulder.

"It's okay. I'm just getting you some water."

Now that he's mentioned it, my mouth is parched. I lick my cracked lips and look around for my pink hiking pack. My trusty lip gloss is never far from my reach. "Excuse me," I call to the Viking. "Do you have my things?"

"Yep." He re-enters the bedroom with a glass of water in one hand and my pink pack in the other. "This pack would be impossible to miss. Surprised you're not blinded by that color," he grunts, handing me my bag.

"Pink is my favorite color." I dig around and find my phone. The screen has gone black and the glass is cracked. Oh well. First things first. I pull out my lip gloss and apply it twice, smacking my lips. When I look up, the Viking is staring at my lips with a look of hunger, making all the blood in my body rush to my face.

"Thanks." I gulp down the water he hands me to hide my fluster. In my haste, I spill some on my chest and have to brush the droplets off my boobs before it soaks in. My nipples are so hard, they poke through three layers of clothing. *Stop it*, I tell them. *This is not a wet t-shirt contest.*

Is it too much to hope the Viking did not see this? I sneak a look.

Yes, yes it is. He saw everything.

I take another sip of water and spill it on myself again. "I have a drinking problem," I quip. "Don't mind me."

The Viking clears his throat and jerks his gaze away. "What's your name?" he asks.

I stiffen. "How did you say I got here?"

"Easy," he says in a soothing voice. "You're safe. I found you on the trail. You were hurt." He motions to my forehead. "You hit your head."

I touch the bandage, hating how weak I feel. I should be wary of waking up in a strange place with a strange person, even if my instincts say I can trust this Viking. Or at least jump him. Maybe it's not my instincts talking, it's my hormones.

"Did you see my stepbrother? He was hiking with me."

He hesitates before saying, "No."

"That's odd." There's something I need to remember, but it's all hazy, hidden behind a wall of pain. "I'm Lana."

"Lana? I'm Teddy."

"OMG." I drop my hand and grin at him. "Teddy? Like Teddy Bear?"

My smile seems to fluster him. "Teddy Medvedev, actually. Did you just say *OMG* out loud?"

"Oh...um, yeah." My nervousness has dropped away, leaving me giddy. This is the guy who picked out the curtains. I didn't expect a sexy mountain man, but anyone who decorates with cute little bears is automatically a friend. "This is your cabin."

"Yes." He watches me warily. "I brought you here because you weren't waking up. I figured you needed rest. I got a doctor to check you out—"

"You did?"

"Yeah. He bandaged your head but said to let you rest."

"I can't believe I slept through all that. Um, thanks for all the help."

"Of course." He's still studying me like he wishes he could see my thoughts. "Where are you from, Lana?"

I like the way he says my name. "I live in L.A. I came here to hike to the summit and scatter my parents' ashes. See?" I proffer my trail mix as proof.

He peers into the bag. "Almonds and M&M's." His tone holds a question.

"My patented blend," I say. "No, seriously, I'm thinking of patenting it. I could sell it in stores. I bet it would fly off the shelves."

Unlike Bentley, Teddy doesn't scoff. He reaches in, takes out a handful and chomps on it thoughtfully. "It's good."

"See?" I beam at him. "I told you."

He takes another handful. "Do you remember anything else about your hike?"

"Not really. Just leaving the rental car and... trying to reach the summit with Bentley."

"Bentley?"

"My stepbrother. Named after the car."

Teddy stops eating trail mix long enough to make a face.

"I know, right? Who names their kid after a car? Even if it is a nice car. Although I'm named after a bimbo in the sitcom *Three's Company*," I inform him, "which isn't much better. Especially when your stepbrother uses it to make fun of you."

Teddy finishes all my trail mix. He crumples up the bag like it offended him. "That's not very nice." His voice is a low rumble, almost a growl.

"Oh, Bentley isn't nice," I agree. "I swear, he'd be happy if a bad bear came out of the woods to eat me." My head aches again. "Wait, I think I just remembered something."

"Yes?" Teddy sits carefully on the edge of the bed, near me. His weight makes the mattress dip, and I end up leaning towards him.

I lower my voice to a whisper. "When you rescued me, did you happen to see the 'pizzly' bear?"

"The what?"

"The 'pizzly' bear," I repeat. "You know how polar bears and grizzly bears have started breeding together?"

Teddy opens and closes his mouth several times before saying, "We're nowhere near the habitat of polar bears."

"But because of climate change, their territory is changing. And they're mating with grizzly bears. Polar bears plus grizzlies make 'pizzly' bears. You can call them 'grolar' bears if you prefer."

"I don't...have a preference. Lana, there's no such thing—"

"They're real," I insist. "They're big and meaner than regular bears. I learned all about this on Mamadou Ndiaye's TikTok. He called them Nesquik bears."

Teddy rubs a rough hand over his beard and rises.

I cock my head up at him. "Where are you going?"

"To call the doctor. I think you hit your head harder than I thought."

"No, I'm always goofy. That's why Bentley says the name fits."

His grouchy expression softens. "I'm going to call anyway." He points a finger at me. "Don't leave the cabin. And don't move."

"I was thinking about running a triathlon, but okay." I lie back on the bed then reconsider. "Wait!"

"What?" He pokes his head back in, looking annoyed even though his tone is gentle.

"Can I at least use the bathroom?"

"Of course. It's right there." He motions to the door next to the wardrobe. "Do you need help?"

"No," I say, even though I'm struggling to scoot across the bed.

"C'mere." He bundles me into his arms so fast, I squeak in surprise. I throw my arm around his neck.

I'm a big girl, but he lifts me easily. I breathe in his masculine, woodsy scent and my ovaries drop another hundred eggs. The ache in my head makes it loll onto his shoulder, which feels solid and sturdy.

Especially when he doesn't immediately put me down. He carries me into the bathroom, which is a modern addition to the cabin, bigger than the bedroom. There's a large sink and a separate room for the toilet, and a bathtub with jets in front of bay windows, perfect for soaking and enjoying a view of the forest.

"Wow." I don't lift my head from his shoulder because it's too darn heavy. My head—not his shoulder. "This bathroom is nice." Oops, that was rude. I shouldn't sound so surprised. "Not that the cabin isn't nice. I love the decor. Tiny bears for the win."

He grunts and just stands there, holding me, my head nested against his shoulder. Is he swaying slightly from side to side?

Maybe he's right. I hit my head harder than we both thought because this scenario seems a bit hard to believe.

Giant, gorgeous Viking rocking me gently in his dreamy bathroom?

It can't be.

I lift my head, and he lets me down on the tile. He's so tall, I only come up to his collarbone. I'm the perfect height to study the swell of his pecs under his shirt. What I wouldn't give to see him shirtless. Just the thought makes me dizzy.

Teddy frowns. His big hands are on my arms, steadying me. "You okay, babygirl?"

"Yeah, thanks." I lift my face, and we lock gazes. His grey eyes darken, and hunger flits over his expression. For me?

"You sure?"

I rub my lips together, and his eyes track the movement. "Um, yeah. Thanks for carrying me. I think I've got it from here."

"I'm going to make that call," he says, but doesn't move.

"You smell good," I blurt.

He just nods like it makes perfect sense. "You smell better."

O. M. G. I think he *does* like me.

He takes what appears to be a reluctant step backward. "Okay. Holler if you need me."

"Yep. I will. Thanks."

He shuts the door behind him, and I sigh. Literally.

Now that I'm on my feet, I feel a little steadier. I do my business and examine my freshly bandaged head in the mirror. Teddy's doctor did a good job. But now I need to figure out what happened and where Bentley is.

First things first. That glass of water only made me thirstier. I hobble out to the bedroom on my own. No sign of Teddy, so I poke my head out into the main part of the cabin. There's a fireplace on one wall with a couch and slouchy chair facing it. To the right is the front door, hanging open. The light streaming in from the front windows makes me squint. I lean against the door frame to get my bearings.

Beyond the sitting area is a small kitchen, galley shaped with lots of pine cabinets and a black wood stove. Someone's standing in front of the open fridge, hunched over, rummaging around. Bottles clink.

"Teddy?" I call.

The figure straightens, and all the breath leaves my lungs. Fuzzy ears, black fur, long snout. That's not Teddy.

There's a bear in the kitchen.

3

Teddy

I've got a human in my house. A *cute* human. She remembers the bear, but if she saw me shift, she's not saying.

She doesn't seem to remember everything. Not the hike up to the summit, nor her stepbrother's lame ass attempt at murder.

I don't know why I held back the information about her stepbrother. I could've explained that he was trying to push her off the mountain, and when he saw me he ran off, but it seemed cruel to inflict on someone who just woke up with a head injury. But I can't coddle her forever. She needs to know the truth. As long as her stepbrother's still out there, she's in danger.

That's okay, my bear says contentedly. *We'll protect her.*

I rub both hands over my face. This is not a complication I need. But like it or not, I have a human for a guest, and my protective instinct is going crazy. I need to keep her safe, monitor her symptoms. And I need to feed her.

Humans eat eggs, right? The Terrible Threes keep

their chickens nearby, even though I told them time and time again to move them closer to Ma's cabin. My younger brothers are terrible at doing their chores, so there are probably plenty of eggs ready for me to collect.

I call Matthias as I hustle down to the coops, and he tells me to give Lana some Tylenol and keep her quiet for the rest of the night. I end the call and chase off Big Bertha, the mean hen, so I can collect my guest's dinner.

I'm on my way back, my arms full of eggs, when I pick up the scent of an intruder. The front door of my cabin is open and swinging in the breeze. "Motherfucker…"

I pick up my pace, dropping a few eggs as I rush into the cabin. I make it just in time to hear Lana's gasp. She's standing in the bedroom door, her mouth hanging open. In the kitchen is a big black bear, its face stuck into my ice box.

"No!" I snap and wave my arms, forgetting I'm carrying the eggs. Several more splatter to the floor. I catch two of them and lob them at the bear. It scuttles back but gets a yolk to the snout. Snuffing and sneezing, it shakes its head, spraying egg everywhere.

"Out." I charge forward, keeping myself between the bear and Lana. I wave an arm like a traffic cop, gesturing to the door. The bear, who is really my brother Axel, gives me a reproachful look and ambles towards the exit. Halfway there, he stops and swivels his head towards my bedroom. He's scented Lana.

"Now!" I bellow, getting behind him, so I can herd him out. The idiot's probably hungover and looking for easy grub in my fridge. Goddammit. I should've put out word that I was on a top secret mission not to be disturbed.

By the time I get Axel out, my floor is covered in oozing egg yolks and broken shells. Both the fridge and the freezer doors are hanging open, and I have to shove a bunch of food back in to close them. One frozen package is pierced with claw marks—some deer sausage Axel made last year. He made so much, he had to store the extra with me. I'd forgotten it was there.

There are three small eggs that survived the fight. If I salvage them and the pack of sausage, I can make the human female a full meal.

Oh, shit, the female.

Lana is still standing in the door, her brown eyes wide and staring. I hustle over to her.

"Lana." I rest my hands on her shoulders and check her over. "You okay? Talk to me."

Her lower lip trembles. "B-b-b—"

"Bear." I gather her into my arms. This is the third time today I've held her, and damn if it doesn't get better every time. "Yes, I know. He's gone now." I raise my voice and holler out the window at Axel's retreating form. "And he won't come back."

"He just wandered in through the door and got into the fridge," Lana is breathless. "Guess the bears really are bad around here."

"You have no idea."

I scoop her up and set her on the couch. "The doctor said I should keep you quiet tonight." She curls into a ball, still looking traumatized. What else do humans need to be comfortable? I grab a blanket and tuck it around her. I can make a fire, but I need to collect logs. First I need to clean up. I rush to do that, making sure the front door stays closed. I don't want any more brothers wandering in.

"Was that him?" Lana asks. "Was that the resident bad bear? He looks different from the one I saw at the summit. That one was brown."

I toss logs into the fireplace and set the extra on their pallet by the wood stove. "No, that was a different one.

He's...he's harmless. If he comes in again, just wave him off."

She blinks. "That was incredible. You just chased him out." She makes shooing motions. "Like swatting a fly."

I grunt. Deep down, my bear preens. "Like I said, he's harmless."

"You were so brave. Like Bear Gryllis. Do you know him?"

"What? No."

"Too bad. He'd be perfect to model my new mountain bear inspired fashion line. So would you, actually. Would you ever consider modeling?"

"Not a chance." I frown at the pyre of kindling. Matthias said to watch for symptoms of concussion. "You know, the doctor said head injuries can cause behavior changes. Are you—"

"Oh, I'm always like this." She waves a hand. "My brain jumps around and can't sit still. Bentley says I'm feeble-minded."

"Bentley." I growl the name, and she laughs softly. It instantly becomes a sound I crave hearing again and again.

"You sound like you've met him."

"No. Not yet."

And he won't like it when I do.

"I'm going to get you some Tylenol and ice for your head. Hang on a second, babygirl."

She twists her head to follow me with her gaze as I go to the kitchen to retrieve a bag of frozen blueberries for her head. I return with a glass of water, the Tylenol, and the blueberries.

A smart bear would just hand her the things and get back. Keep his distance from the alluring human.

I guess I'm not a smart bear. I'm definitely a bad bear.

Because I crouch beside my guest and apply the blueberry pack myself.

It's not because I want another deep drink of her honey scent. Definitely not because I can't get enough of her chirpy conversation or alluring pink braids. It's more that my bear insists on taking care of her.

Although now I'm torn between lifting her onto my lap to cradle her head and apply the icepack and feeding her dinner.

But this is nuts.

I need to back away. Stop touching her. Get my bear under control. I force myself to stand and clear my throat.

"I'm going to clean up the mess in the kitchen and make you some dinner."

"Do you need some help?" the sweet human asks.

"No, babygirl. You lie on that couch and rest." I point a stern finger. "Doctor's orders. And mine."

I swear to Christ, her thighs slap together at my tone, like it turns her on that I'm getting bossy.

My dick instantly gets rock hard for her, and that's before I catch the sweet scent of her arousal.

Oh, damn. It's going to be a very, very long night.

∼

LANA

Teddy mops up the egg mess with a wet cloth and then uses a real mop to finish the job. For a huge mountain man, he's more than capable with a mop. Quick and efficient. Graceful, despite his size.

"What do you do for a living, Teddy?"

"Helicopter pilot."

"Really?" I sit up taller to get a better look at him with

that career in mind. I was picturing more like lumberjack or firejumper. Pilot is hot, too, though.

"Rest." He points that finger at me again. The one that makes my internal muscles tighten and my panties get damp.

As the CEO of my own company and a multi-millionaire, not to mention a plus-sized woman, I do a lot of the bossing around. Is it wrong to be turned on by a guy who is bigger and stronger and far more dominant than I am for a change?

I smile. "What made you choose that career?"

Teddy shrugs. "I didn't choose it. The Army chose it for me."

"Ah, military guy. I should've guessed by that barrel chest."

Teddy looks down at his chest with his brows furrowed. He gives his head a shake. "I'm going to feed you now. And then you're going back to bed. Early night."

"Yes, Daddy," I say suggestively. He can daddy me any time. All the time. With alacrity.

He arches a brow, and I press my legs together to hide my quiver.

"Do you want eggs and sausage? Or something less greasy?"

I pull the bag of frozen blueberries off my head. "Can I eat these?"

"Yes. But that's not a meal." He takes the bag and heads to the kitchen. After some rummaging in the cupboards and his icebox, he returns with a bowl of blueberries in what looks like ice cream. "It's milk. My mom used to make this for us. Frozen blueberries in milk. The cold freezes the milk, turns it purple."

"It's delicious." I chip away at the icy milk.

"Go slowly. Don't get brain freeze." He sits near me,

and once again, his weight on the couch makes me lean into him.

"My mom used to give me ice cream when I was sick," I say between bites. "After she met Roger, they were really busy, but the nanny did the same thing. At least, she did before I went off to boarding school."

"How old were you when your mom met Roger?"

"I was eight. Bentley was ten. Mom and Roger were really in love, and I was happy for them. She is a stage actress, and he cast her in a few movies. They met on set. She's really beautiful… I mean, she *was* beautiful."

"I'm sorry for your loss."

"It's okay. My parents weren't super present in my life. I've been grieving the loss of them since I was young, honestly. Besides, they died doing what they love. Flying to Cabo."

Teddy's brows slam down. "Was that a joke?"

"Um, yeah. Kinda." I set the bowl aside and lick my cold lips. "Are my lips blue?"

"Purple." Teddy's gaze locks onto them, and he leans forward, close to me. "You have a bit of…" His voice is low and gravelly. His tongue flicks out against my lower lip, and I suck in my breath. "Ice there," he explains.

I lean forward to press my mouth against his, desperate for the kiss I thought was coming.

He groans and catches the back of my head to hold me in place. When he kisses me back, I feel it everywhere– tingles that spin and dance across my skin. A pulsing between my legs. A shiver across my collarbones.

But my head also throbs, and I grow dizzy. I let out an involuntary whimper, and Teddy pulls back. "Sorry." He coughs. "You're hurt. I don't know what I was thinking."

For one terrible moment, I think he's going to get up and leave, but instead he puts the bowl on the coffee table and turns me, so my legs are draped over his. I guess we're done making out now. That's disappointing but for the best. The pounding in my head eases with every rise and fall of his chest.

When he starts talking, his voice is so low and soothing, I find myself sinking deeper into his hold. "When I was seven, my Ma adopted my brother and me."

I hold very still, waiting for him to say more.

"Our biological mom had us young. She wasn't expecting kids. Didn't quite know what to do with us. We were raised in a van, always traveling around, camping. She taught us how to live wild. Then one year, she decided we were old enough to be able to look after ourselves, so she dumped us here on Bad Bear Mountain and took off."

I press my lips together to keep my mouth from hanging open. My parents liked to travel too, but they hired a nanny to watch Bentley and me when they were jet setting. Who abandons their kids in the middle of the woods when they're barely out of kindergarten?

"She used to be in a commune with Ma on this mountain," Teddy continues. "So she thought we'd be all right. But the commune had dissolved. Only Ma was still here. She found us sleeping in a ragged tent. Coaxed us into her cabin with chocolate chip cookies and built us bunk beds."

"That's…" I don't know what to say. It's awful how he and his brother were abandoned. And incredible what their Ma did. "I'm glad she found you."

"Yeah, me too. Around the same time, she took in my other brother, Matthias when both his parents died. The thing is, she'd always wanted kids, but she wasn't in a relationship. After that, she adopted triplets. She took us all in."

I blink back the heat behind my eyes. My estimation of Teddy's Ma goes from Wonder Woman to Goddess.

"Matthias was the good brother. He's always had his head on straight. Darius and I were half wild. Always fighting. I think we took our rage out on each other."

"I can imagine. Teddy, that's…" I still don't know what to say. "I can't believe you went through all that."

"Yeah. Don't talk about it much. Or at all."

"I get that."

He absently squeezes my knee, and I put my hand over his big, rough one. We sit for a while like that, holding hands like it's the most natural thing in the world. Like I didn't just meet this guy today under the strangest of circumstances.

A yawn overtakes me—so big my jaw cracks. I try to hide it, but Teddy sees.

"All right, babygirl. Time for bed."

"What? Already?" The sun has set while we were talking.

"C'mon." He scoops me up. I'm a big girl, but this giant Viking lifts and carries me effortlessly. Seriously, he must do biceps curls with tree trunks. I throw my arm around his neck and enjoy the ride.

"You know," I say as he carries me to the bedroom. "I could get used to this. You carrying me. I'm sorry I missed it the first time. Being unconscious and all."

He eases me down to the floor. "Yeah, about that. I wouldn't have moved you except–"

"Oh I'm not mad. I'm just sorry I missed our first cuddle."

"What? No. There was no cuddling."

"I'm just teasing you. Although I'm sure you give good cuddles, even if it'd be a little scratchy. Cause, you know, your beard."

Teddy cocks his head, staring at me like I'm some sort of strange new creature.

"Your beard is so big, it looks like it chews up razors and spits them out." Acting on impulse, I reach out and touch the overgrown bristle on his chin. "Oooh, it's soft. I didn't expect that. You know, because your Resting Murderer face."

"Okay, enough." He catches my hand but doesn't pull away. "You need rest."

"Night, Viking." I stroke his jaw again. "Nighty-night, Viking's beard."

He rolls his eyes and points to the bathroom. "There's a new toothbrush still in the packaging in the drawer beside the sink. Borrow anything you like from my closet—if you toss your things out the door, I'll put them through the wash, so they'll be ready by morning. Call me if you need me."

The toothbrush is right where he said it would be. I eagerly open the wardrobe and grab a pair of soft, faded boxers and a t-shirt to sleep in. And damn if they aren't the comfiest thing I've ever put on. The boxers make my ass look cute, so I go with it.

Forget nightgowns and lounge wear. The next line I design for GoddessWear™ is going to be boyfriend-style clothes. Perfect for your man to wear and you to steal.

Once I'm dressed, I crack the door open and peer into the dark cabin. It takes a moment for me to spot my Viking. He's crouched by the hearth, banking the fire.

I pad towards him and set the bundle of my dirty clothes on the coffee table. "Teddy? Where are you going to sleep?"

"On the couch."

Can he even fit on the couch? "But—"

"I'll be fine, babygirl."

It's on the tip of my tongue to ask him to tuck me in, but I've already borrowed the man's clothes and stolen his bed, so I leave the door open and settle into bed. The pillows hold Teddy's scent. I've never been into a guy's smell before, but Teddy's is divine. Fresh mountain air, something herbal like rosemary, and salt from sweat. Good sweat that comes from a long run in the forest followed by an epic sex marathon.

And now I'm horny. Scratch that, I've been horny since our moment on the couch. The couch Teddy is crammed on right now...

I roll to the left, then to the right. I can't get comfortable. If I'm not comfortable, Teddy's gotta be suffering, too.

"Teddy?"

"I'm here." His voice is a lot closer than I expected, coming from just outside the door. "You're not sleeping."

His shadow figure is in the doorway. I hold my hand out to him, and he comes in and takes it. He moves silently for such a big guy.

"I'm not feeling well," I say.

"You're not?"

I squeeze my eyes shut and remember my daily affirmations. *Be brave. Ask for what you want.*

I clear my throat. "I've got a fever. And the only prescription is more cuddles."

"Is that so, babygirl?" His head is bowed, but I hear a smile in his voice.

"Yes. It is so."

"All right. Scoot over."

Squee!

His weight dips the bed, and he positions me where he wants me, in front of him, on my side facing the wardrobe. The bed is big, but so is Teddy, and for us both to fit, he has to wrap himself around me.

Which is not a hardship. At all. I'd trade all my dates

with lame highschool boyfriends for a ten minute Teddy snuggle.

"This comfortable?" he asks.

"Yes. You're a good cuddler." I can't stop my excited wriggle. After a few seconds of squirming, Teddy tightens his grip around me.

"None of that."

"Okay." I try to fall asleep, but I can't stop giggling.

His sigh gusts over the back of my neck. "What is it now?"

"I was just thinking. You're so big, you have your own gravitational pull. Whenever you sit next to me, I fall into you."

Silence.

I wait for him to answer and get nervous when he doesn't. "That's okay, right?"

"Yeah. Now go to sleep."

So bossy. But he's warm and holding me the way I want, so instead of arguing, I do as he says.

4

Teddy

Six a.m. sharp, I open my eyes. There's a robin outside my window shrieking its head off. It's overly-excited because it's spring, and it's trying to attract a mate and get laid.

Me too, crazy bird. Me too.

Lana is a warm, sleeping bundle tucked into my body. We spent the night together, me leaving only twice, once to check the perimeter and once to put her wet clothes in the dryer. I slept in my jeans, but my cock is doing its best to punch through the denim to nestle itself in the sweet, sweet crevice of Lana's ass.

With a groan, I pull away from her sexy perfection and extricate myself from the blankets. My dick is so hard, I walk stiff legged to the bathroom and close the door. A few minutes stroking my dick, picturing Lana's glorious curves, and I'm spilling over my hand like a teenager.

But when I open the door and get a face full of Lana's honeyed scent, my dick turns to steel all over again. It didn't even take the edge off, but it'll have to do.

I step out into the cool dawn and pull out my phone. I fire off a few texts—one to my brother Matthias, letting him know his patient had a good night, and he should come by and check on her. Another one to my friend Rafe Lightfoot in Taos. Rafe is alpha of the Black Wolf pack. He and his whole pack were in my unit in the Army, and now they run a security operation that allows them to run black ops missions on the side. If they can't track Lana's shithead stepbrother, no one can.

I borrow Lana's pack to dig out her driver's license and shoot a picture of it to Rafe. Lana's still sleeping, her breathing even. She probably won't wake for a while, but when she does, she'll be hungry. I need to get supplies. Luckily the Bad Bear Trading Post is open at the crack of dawn.

On my way into town, Matthias rings back.

"How's the patient?" My doctor brother sounds alert for the early hour. He's like me, an early riser.

"She's healing."

"Does she remember anything?"

"I don't know."

"I got a message to the leech in Las Cruces. He's on standby."

I bare my teeth. That's the same vampire who mind-wiped Tiffany. From what I remember, he enjoyed the irony of living in a town called "The Crosses." Leech humor is weird.

"The sooner we do it, the fewer memories we'll have to take," Matthias continues. He sounds so practical. I want to punch him.

The thought of mind wiping the beautiful woman in my bed makes me sick. What if it messes her up? What if it changes her thinking patterns or her sunny personality?

It could turn her into a different person. It could ruin her life.

And selfishly, I don't want her to forget about me.

But the alternative is worse. "What are the chances she'll just forget what she saw for good?"

"The healing serum I gave her is powerful. Sooner or later, she'll remember everything."

Damn.

Matthias lets the silence stretch. When it's clear I'm not going to say anything, he asks, "Do you want me to do it? After my patients today, I could pick her up and take her."

"No." I blow out a breath, bracing myself and forcing the image of Lana lying peacefully in my bed out of my mind. I had her in my arms for one night. It'll have to be enough. "When it's time to mindwipe her, I'll do it myself."

∼

LANA

Once again, the cute curtains greet me as soon as I open my eyes. The bears are dancing in the breeze, letting in the strong morning light. I feel like a bulldozer ran over me, but in a good way. There's no sharp pain in my head, and I'm woozy like I spent most of the night in a deep sleep.

I'm alone, but there's a mountain man-sized dent in the bed next to me. Evidence that Teddy spent the whole night beside me. He must have woken up early and let me sleep in.

"Teddy?" I roll out of bed, yawning. I'm still in his boxers and t-shirt, but my freshly washed clothes have magically appeared on the foot of the bed. The morning is chilly, so I put on my pink pants. I swap the t-shirt for my camisole and snag a plaid shirt to cover my arms. The sleeves hang over my wrists until I roll them up, but I can't button it over my breasts. If I'm staying here much longer, I'll need clothes.

And how much longer am I going to be staying here? Yesterday, I was out of it, but I should figure out how to find Bentley and get off this mountain. Get out of Teddy's hair. I at least need to get my phone fixed and charged.

The cabin is empty. No sign of Teddy in the kitchen or living room. At least there's no bear. I'm not sure I'm up to shooing away a bear before coffee. Or in this lifetime.

I step out of the cabin. Without a helicopter landing in the meadow, the grasses and wildflowers are pretty as a picture on a postcard. I'd snap a photo if my phone wasn't as cracked as my head.

Man, I've been through a lot in the last twenty-four hours. Hiked a mountain, hit my head, lost my stepbrother, got rescued by a sexy mountain man and ensconced in his cabin... There's too much to even recount. Cuddles with Teddy were the high point. My head injury and forgetting how it happened is the low. Bear sightings, including a bear raiding Teddy's refrigerator, are somewhere in the middle.

I'm also worried about my brother. I'd be more frantic about finding him if I deep down didn't believe that he simply abandoned me and hiked down without me. I'll give him the benefit of the doubt and assume he left before I hit my head.

Hmmm.

All these thoughts are dark, and it's a beautiful day. I'm in a field full of happy flowers. I spent the night in the arms of a mountain man. For now, I can pretend I'm on vacation. I'll deal with the rest later.

I wade deeper into the field, shielding my eyes from the sun. I could attempt a *Sound of Music* montage, complete with twirling, but that might not be good for my head, so I settle for a gentle stroll, following a path through the grasses towards the treeline. Beyond the copse of pines, there's a row of wooden boxes. A few more steps, and I hear a humming sound. Bees. The boxes are beehives.

There's a shadowy shape moving among them. I shield my eyes, about to call Teddy's name, when the figure lumbers into view.

It's a bear, the biggest one I've ever seen. Its fur is dappled in shadow, but its paws are clearly outlined as it picks up the top of a beehive and places it—crawling with bees—on another hive. Bees hover in the air around the bear's head. Some of them land on its fur, but they don't seem angry. The bear's movements are slow and calm as it shuffles the boxes of beehives around.

I rub my eyes. Is this really happening? I've stopped short in the cluster of trees, unable to walk, unwilling to run and draw the bear's attention to me.

The bear sees me anyway and rears up on its hind paws. It's still in shadow, so I can't tell if it's brown or black or a pizzly bear. Not that the color of its fur matters. If the bear wants to eat me, I'm dead either way.

For a long moment, the bear and I stare at each other with the bees buzzing between us.

The bear waves a huge paw at me and drops to all fours then lumbers off into the forest beyond the beehives.

I sag against a tree trunk. Teddy's right. I must have hit my head harder than I thought.

"Lana!" Teddy storms out from behind the cabin.

"Teddy," I say weakly.

He snatches me up and heads back to the cabin. "You can't be out here, it's too dangerous."

"I know." I clutch his neck tight. His beard chafes my forehead, and it feels just right.

Once we're back in the cabin, I get over my shock. "I

just saw a bear trying to get honey out of the beehives back there. You should've seen it, Teddy. It was different from the others. I didn't see its fur, but it was huge. It had to be a pizzly bear."

Teddy grunts and puts me down on the couch. "Are you okay?"

"I'm not hurt."

He's patting me down, so I catch his hands. "This is incredible. I can't believe no one's done a nature show on this mountain."

Teddy pulls away. "No shows. We like our privacy."

"I get it. But it's a shame no one's done even one documentary. This place is a national treasure. It's almost as if the bears around here act like people."

Teddy has paced to the door. He pushes it shut and stands in the shadows, rubbing the back of his neck.

"Are you okay?" I ask.

He doesn't answer. Was it something I said?

It's funny, I can let Bentley's rejection roll off my back, but Teddy's bothers me. I draw my knees up to my chest.

Teddy's head is bowed, but I sense his agitation. It must have been something I said. Or did.

"I should probably get going. Get out of your hair. Get back to my business."

"No," he barks.

"No?" I blink at him.

He returns to my side as swiftly as he left. Once he gets close, he doesn't seem to know what to do, so he grabs the blanket and tucks it around me. "You need to stay here and rest." His gentle tone makes me relax.

"I think I'm pretty well rested. I should at least make a plan for today. Do you have a phone I could use? An iPhone charger?"

"Why?"

"To make some calls. Check in at work. Check around. If anything, I should figure out what happened to Bentley. I feel like a bad sister, lounging around while he could be lost on the mountain. Or worse. What if he hit his head too?"

"He's not on the mountain. I had Matthias and my brothers who do search and rescue scour the mountain for him. If he's here, he's hidden well. It's more likely that he's left. I have a team working on tracking him."

"A team? That sounds serious."

"Sorry babygirl, I don't want to scare you. He's probably fine. "

"Yeah, he probably is. Maybe we had a falling out before I hit my head, and that's why he left me."

Teddy opens his mouth, then closes it and squeezes my hand. "Yeah." He clears his throat. "That could be."

"Bentley's always been rough with me. I seem to get on his every nerve by just existing." I shrug because as much as I don't want that to be true, as much as I'd love it not to be true, when I'm honest with myself, I know it just is. I can still make the best of right now. "Well, I can at least get into town and find a way to charge my phone. Or fix it. I'm not up to hiking to the summit, but a gentle stroll back down to a place where I can catch a ride—"

I trail off because Teddy's shaking his head.

"Or do you have a car I can borrow? I'm a good driver."

"No car."

"A bike? A burro? A golf cart retrofitted with ATV tires?"

He's still shaking his head. "Nope."

"Oh well, guess I'll have to walk." I rise to my feet and sashay to the door, testing something.

I don't get more than five feet away from the couch before Teddy scoops me up and drags me back.

"Just as I suspected." I plant my finger in his chest. His pecs are so firm, I bend my finger. "You don't want me to leave."

"You're hurt," he growls.

After years of Bentley's cruelty and my parents' indifference, his concern makes me feel all melty inside. And fuels my inner sunshine. My cells seem to pulse light as I'm cuddled in this gorgeous Viking's arms. How did I get so lucky? Like seriously, what happened?

"I'm an important woman. Things to do. Places to see." I push at him with a bit of flirt, torn between wanting to be productive and wanting to stay right here in his arms forever, but he doesn't budge. "Seriously, Teddy, how long do you think you can keep me here?" I blink up at him, really looking into his eyes, wondering who is this kind Viking and where he's been all my life.

His eyes flash with a bright color. It's there one moment, gone the next. Must be a trick of the light. "As long as I want to."

Long. Yeah, that works for me. Let's see if he really means it.

"Oh yeah? We'll see about that." While holding his gaze, I turn, 'accidentally' planting my backside in his lap and wriggling around until he growls and grips my hips.

"Lana," he warns.

"Viking," I answer, my core clenching so tightly, he's got to feel my body responding. I bite my lip, hoping he does.

He tips me onto my back on the couch and leans over me with his hand planted next to my head. "You're not leaving. I mean it."

"You can't stop me," I whisper back, thrilled with this new game.

"Try me." He rests his weight on me, not all of it, but just enough to keep me pinned and let me feel his erection, which feels like a giant compass needle pointing me to true north. Heaven.

"I'll run away when you're not looking."

He nuzzles along my face. His beard scratches deliciously along my soft cheek. "I'll tie you to my bed."

My insides seize. "I might like that." My voice comes out strangled.

"Oh yeah, babygirl? Then I might have to think up some other ways to punish you."

O. M. G. "Promise?"

He slants his head and kisses me. Heat flares between us. His hand is under my thigh, massaging, promising me to touch me in other ways. I grab him, tugging him down. I want his full weight on me. It might leave a permanent imprint on the couch, but it'd be worth it.

I'm caught up in a daze, hitching myself under Teddy to rub my lower half against him when my stomach growls.

Teddy breaks the kiss and frowns down at me.

"Ignore that?" I ask, even as my stomach snarls again. "Please?"

"I can't." He brushes a final kiss to my mouth and slides off the couch. "I need to feed you." I reach for him with a whine, and he catches my hands, kissing the palms and rising. "Breakfast first."

"Breakfast?"

"Yep, I woke up early to get supplies."

"So that's where you were. I was looking for you."

"I'm sorry, babygirl. I didn't think you'd wake before I got back." He boops my nose and heads to the kitchen, where a new crop of bags has appeared. Groceries. The supplies he went to fetch. For me? "Next time, I'll leave a note."

Next time? I wrap my arms around myself in a butterfly hug and angle my head to hide my smile.

Teddy pads around the kitchen, unloading eggs and milk and setting out a huge cast iron griddle that covers half the stove top.

I wander closer, enjoying this sight of a big Viking being domestic. "Can I help?"

"Naw, I got this."

I walk to the door and hover on the stoop. I'm not very fast, but if I'm very quiet, maybe I can sneak away…

It's a test. I don't really want to leave but am curious about how far my Viking will take his threat to keep me here.

My foot hits a creaky floorboard.

"Don't even think about it," Teddy says without looking up.

I whirl and prop my hands on my hips. "So that's it? I'm just your prisoner?"

"Yep." He smirks. He's enjoying this way too much.

I narrow my eyes at him. He doesn't want me to leave, and he's not telling me why. He didn't try anything last night, much to my disappointment.

Although I admit, it probably wouldn't have gone well with my achy head.

"Sit," he orders, and I obey, returning to the couch. Even if I could've snuck away, Teddy is insanely fast. He would catch me before I crossed the meadow.

Teddy bangs pots and pans in the kitchen. "I'm making you pancakes. Do you like pancakes?"

"Everyone likes pancakes."

"And bacon." He pulls out brown paper packages wrapped in butcher twine. "I got five pounds of bacon."

"That's a lot of bacon."

"Everyone loves bacon."

I touch the bandage on my head. "I should be making plans to go, though. At least find somewhere I can fix my phone. Or charge it."

"No."

"Why not?"

"Because the doctor said you needed rest."

Hmmmm. He could be worried about my head injury. Or he could be keeping me here because of something else. Something besides what's sizzling between us.

That's okay. I'll just wear out my welcome. Time for Operation Annoy Teddy to commence. "Well, now's a good time to tell you that I'm vegan."

Teddy raises his head from the counter where he's unwrapping the bacon. "Seriously?"

"Oh yes. No exceptions."

"Not even bacon?"

My stomach gurgles. In a minute, he's going to be frying bacon, and I'm not going to be able to resist. "Except for bacon," I amend and think hard about the ingredients of pancakes, since I said I'd eat them. "And milk. And butter. And baking soda." Is baking soda an animal product? "And the occasional rib-eye," I add, just to be safe. If Teddy makes steaks, I'm not passing my portion up.

"So what you're saying is, you're a bad vegan."

I spread my hands in an idk gesture. "See how annoying it will be to have me around?"

"You say *annoying*. I say *cute*."

"Cute?" I prop my fists on my hips, but inside I'm *squee*ing.

"Mhmm." He goes back to prepping breakfast.

"Well maybe, I'll think up a way to be a bad house guest. The bears will have nothing on me."

He points a spatula my way. "You keep it up, and I'll spank you before tying you to the bed."

All the air leaves the room. I wheeze and finally find enough oxygen to squeak. "Promise?"

"You know it, babygirl." He shoots a look across the room that makes my toes curl. All the water in my body is heading between my legs to make my panties damp.

I collapse back on the couch and pull a pillow over my face. I'll hide here until I get my composure.

Teddy smirks as he bustles about the kitchen. He thinks he's won. Seems like being an annoying house guest isn't going to work.

Holy crap, am I seriously being abducted by some hot guy? Is he just being nice and seducing me, and then I'm going to wake up tied to the bed, and he's going to go all Kathy Bates *Misery* on me? If this fine ass man is just going to woo me and keep me hostage so he can kill me and eat me later, I'm going to be so pissed.

Hopefully he's just kind of bossy and concerned?

I nibble my lip and ponder the situation. Nothing about him feels off. In fact, everything about him feels completely safe.

Maybe I can wait another day. Rest up and recover and then fix my phone and find Bentley.

I mean, I wouldn't mind another shot at getting horizontal with my sexy Viking. My libido agrees with this plan. After breakfast, Operation Jump Teddy's Bones will officially begin.

5

Teddy

A sharp rap on the door makes me whirl, but it's only Matthias.

"Hello." My brother steps in, ducking his head for the low ceiling. "I see the patient is feeling better."

"Hi." Lana gives a little wave.

Suddenly I find myself between her and my brother.

Behind me, Lana gasps. "Holy wow, Teddy. You move so fast."

Matthias's brows knit together.

I did it again. I'm losing it in front of a human. What is happening?

"Teddy?" my brother says. He steps to move past me and an unbidden growl lodges in my throat.

Mine. My bear says. *Mate.*

Shit.

~

Lana

Teddy is in some sort of staring match with the tall man who just walked in. The newcomer is clean-shaven, in slacks and a button down, carrying a big black leather bag. He looks like a missionary coming door-to-door.

"Teddy?" Something is off with me. I don't like doctors, plus I feel skittish after the little bear-in-the kitchen incident, and I want my Viking close. I hold out a hand for him, and he comes over, folding himself onto the couch next to me.

"It's okay," he says. "Lana, this is the doctor."

The tall man blinks at me owlishly through his round glasses. "Lana? I'm Matthias," he says in a deep voice. "I examined you earlier."

"Thanks," I whisper. My head throbs sharply. I press closer to Teddy.

The doctor follows my every movement. "You feeling okay?"

"Her head hurts," Teddy rumbles. He eases me into his lap. "It's okay, babygirl."

I love that he calls me babygirl. It makes me feel as warm and gooey as a fresh-baked chocolate chip cookie.

"I'm okay." I curl into Teddy's warmth and give Matthias a brave smile. "I'm just not the biggest fan of doctors."

"Understandable." Matthias sets down his bag on the pine coffee table. "I'm not big fan of going to the doctor myself."

"Matthias is my brother," Teddy murmurs into my ear.

"Oh." I look from Teddy's tanned face to Matthias, who is a few shades darker than I am.

"We're adopted," Matthias says.

"Oh yes. Six of you, right?"

Teddy shrugs. "Seven or eight."

"Seven or eight?" I crane my neck to gaze into his grey eyes. "You're not sure?"

"There's so many of us, I lose track. The triplets are identical. That makes it harder."

I gape at him.

"I'm joking, Lana."

"Right," I mumble. I squint up at Matthias in supplication and catch him chasing a smile from his lips.

"Teddy, it's not nice to joke with someone who has a head injury," he chastises.

"Yeah, *Teddy.*" I squirm in Teddy's lap, trying to get comfortable. He clamps his arms around me, his big biceps bracing me. I poke one to check its firmness. Just as I thought–his muscles are rigid without him needing to flex.

When I glance up, both Teddy and the doctor are staring at me.

"Just testing something," I say. "Um, carry on."

"I just want to check your head." Matthias sits on the coffee table in front of me. "Nothing too invasive, I assure you. While you were unconscious yesterday, I cleaned your cut and checked your pupils. I'd like to examine your head for bruising. If all's well, it will be painless."

"Okay." I hold still.

Matthias feels over my head, questioning me when I wince. He shines a light into my eyes and pronounces my pupils fine. "No signs of internal bleeding. And your head cut is healing up."

"That's good." I'm squirming again. It's like there's a big log in his pants and... *Oh.* I stop grinding on his dick. Teddy leans back and takes me with him, cradling me in the curve of one burly arm.

"I think you will make a full recovery. With rest," Matthias says. "No excessive movement today, and no strenuous activity for a while. "

"So no hiking?" I ask to be cheeky.

"Not today."

Crap. I should figure stuff out. My cell is broken, and I should get it fixed and touch base with my staff, but all I want to do is snuggle against Teddy. There is something so comforting about the idea of staying and resting. Like now that Matthias gave me the excuse, I'm happy to run with it.

"Is there any place I can spend the night?"

"Here," Teddy rumbles so loudly, I jolt. "You're staying here."

"Can you stay a few days?" Matthias asks.

"I guess so." I took a week off work. Not that I intended to actually stay off email for a week, but maybe it'll be good for me. I can think up more ideas for the limited edition "Bad Bear" pajamas and sleepwear. What's the point of being the CEO if my team can't run things in my absence?

"Then it's settled. You'll stay here." Teddy squeezes my knee.

Matthias turns his back on us to pack up his doctor's bag, but his cheek is curved like he's quietly laughing at us.

"Thanks for the check up, Doc." I crane my neck to Teddy. "Must be nice, having a medical professional in the family."

Teddy grunts. "Comes in handy when my brothers need a bone set after a fight."

I gasp.

"He's kidding," Matthias assures me, but Teddy looks serious.

"I've always wanted brothers," I say. "Any siblings, really. My stepbrother and I never got along. I tried, but… I think our parents wanted us to get closer… that's why they sent us up the mountain together."

"Matthias is going to keep a look out for your stepbrother." Teddy gives Matthias a meaningful look I can't interpret.

"That's right." Matthias clears his throat. "And we can get the word out to the rest of our brothers."

"Do you all live here on the mountain?"

"Most of us, yes," Matthias says. "I have my own cabin closer to the one where we grew up."

"I called Matthias as soon as I carried you here. He's the one who got your pack. I told him he couldn't miss it."

"Because it's pink." I pick up one of my braids and hold the flamingo colored end up in front of Teddy's face. "My favorite color has its uses."

Teddy shakes his head, so I tease his beard with the end of my braid, to see what he'll do. He lets me tickle him under the chin for two seconds before capturing my hand and pressing it to his chest.

I look back at Matthias, pretending my face isn't flushing. "Did you happen to see an urn up there with it?"

"I saw it," Matthias says after glancing at Teddy. "It was in pieces. I'm sorry, Lana."

"It must have fallen." I go to rub my forehead and remember it's bandaged. "Was it empty?"

Matthias nods.

"So we must have reached the summit." I try to think and am rewarded with a sharp pain in my head. "Ow."

Matthias heads to the kitchen, returning with a glass of water, Tylenol, and more frozen blueberries.

Teddy rubs my back as I take the medicine. "Easy, babygirl. You don't have to deal with it today." He gently holds the cold bag to the back of my neck.

I let myself relax against him. "You're right. Smart Viking."

"Viking?" Matthias coughs to cover a laugh.

"Don't you need to be somewhere?" Teddy snaps at his brother.

"Not really, but I'll head out." Matthias slings his bag over his shoulder. "Daisy sends her regards, by the way. She wants to talk to you before the next town meeting."

"Daisy?" I ask.

"Our mayor," Matthias says. "She's eighty-nine going on fifty."

"Pain in my ass," Teddy mutters.

"Hey." I poke his biceps again. It feels so firm, I do it again. "That's not nice."

"You tell him, Lana," Matthias saunters towards the door, which has creaked open in the breeze again. "Uh, Teddy..."

Teddy tweaks my braids while I poke him in retaliation. "What is it?"

"You need to come see this."

Teddy stiffens, cocking his head towards the door. I sit up. I hear it too–the distant, rhythmic clacking of helicopter blades.

"Sit tight, babygirl." Teddy shifts me carefully onto the couch and strides out the door with Matthias.

I leave the frozen blueberries in a decorative bowl on the coffee table and follow, too curious to stay back. When I reach the door, a gust of wind bangs it open

A helicopter hovers over the grassy meadow in front of Teddy's cabin. Dust flies, pine trees thrash their branches, and wildflowers flatten as it sets down.

I cup my hands over my ears and duck away from the wind. Teddy turns and wraps his arms around me, covering my head with a protective hand.

The helicopter has barely landed when a big man with a black briefcase hops out of the back and waves the pilot away. He strolls towards the cabin as the helicopter lifts off and flies away. I squint but don't recognize the newcomer. In his suit and black sunglasses, he looks like one of the Men In Black.

"Brother," the man calls. He's got blond hair, cut a bit longer than Teddy's and tousled from the helicopter wind. His beard is clipped with surgical precision to line his strong jaw.

The blond business man removes his shades, and I gasp. Take away the suit, the expensive haircut, add worn clothes and a messy beard, and he'd be a mirror image of Teddy.

He sets down the briefcase and holds out his arms. "Miss me?"

Pressed against Teddy's chest, I feel his growl vibrate through me. He carefully maneuvers me aside.

"Teddy," Matthias warns, but Teddy is already storming across the meadow towards his doppleganger.

I sidle up to Matthias. "Is that one of the triplets?" Teddy didn't say he was one of three, but I could've gotten confused.

"No. That's Teddy's twin."

"Darius," Teddy snarls. He prowls up to his twin. With shoulders bunched and hands held away from his sides, he looks like a pit fighter circling his opponent.

"Theodore." Darius the twin folds his glasses and puts them in his pocket. "How are things?"

"Fine. No thanks to you."

"Matthias? And…hello?" A smile spreads across Darius' face when he sees me.

Teddy steps between Darius and me, blocking his twin's line of sight. With them face to face, I get a chance to spot more differences. Teddy has more tattoos. Darius looks like he's ready for the boardroom, Teddy like he just came from a biker rally.

"What are you doing here?" Teddy growls.

"Came to check on things."

"Bullshit. Call back your pilot and get the fuck out of here."

"Theodore," Daruis scoffs in the face of Teddy's rage. I make a note never to call Teddy 'Theodore'. Darius is either really brave or really dumb to keep doing it. "My pilot's halfway to Santa Fe by now. I thought you could give me a ride. Or is Teddy's Helicopter Tours already defunct?"

Teddy shoves his hands in his pockets. "We're on hiatus."

"Pity." Darius is smiling. "I could send you plenty of business. Maybe hire you myself. If I get a family discount."

"You get nothing."

"That's a shame, seeing as I'm here to solve the town's problems. You gonna make me leave before I lay out my proposal? What will Daisy say?"

"She'll say you're full of it. None of us are falling for your bull anymore."

"Fine." Darius steps back. "I'll go as soon as I see Mom."

"Mom doesn't want to see you."

"Are you sure about that brother? Why don't you ask her?"

"We can't ask her, and you know it. It's your fault."

"My fault? You're the one who left. You joined the Army and peaced out. We had to figure it out and guess what? I figured it out."

"You're a fucking sellout," Teddy snarls.

I clap my hand over my mouth. I thought my family had drama, but this is a whole new level. Teddy's about to go nuclear, and judging by the red flush flowing up Darius' neck, he's two seconds away from losing it, too.

"I'm the one who's going to save this mountain. Meanwhile you're hiding here with a female." Darius points at me. This time Matthias steps in front of me, one hand outstretched with the palm towards me, signaling me to keep back.

"Leave her out of this," Teddy says. "You don't look at her. You don't even smell her."

The way Teddy rushes to defend me makes my heart beat faster.

Darius isn't done. "What was the last one's name?"

"You shut your mouth." Teddy's voice is soft.

"Oh that's right." Darius snaps his fingers. "Her name was Tiffany, right? Didn't you learn your lesson about shacking up with hum—"

But I don't get to hear anything more about Tiffany because Teddy's elbow snaps back, and he slams his fist into Darius' face.

~

Teddy

I've been fighting my twin since we were old enough to crawl. My fists know his face better than anyone else's, and his fists know mine. But I've picked up a few tricks since fighting him last.

When I joined the Army, I learned discipline. When Colonel Johnson recruited me into his special team of shifter soldiers, I learned how to fly a warbird into hostile territory, surprise the enemy, and carry out a mission. I learned all sorts of combat styles, but it was between missions, when my unit was bored and our animals needed to blow off steam, that I really learned how to brawl.

Meanwhile Darius went to business school and re-created himself into a soulless mogul. How many fights with another shifter does he have under his belt? He spends all his time with humans who have MBAs.

Underneath that pretty suit, Darius is about my size. His clothes are cut to make him look leaner. It's a good disguise. I underestimated him in the first crucial minutes of our fight and learned the hard way that he still packs a lot of power in his punches.

We circle each other, me with bare feet, him in shiny new shoes that are quickly getting scuffed. My cheek throbs from his last haymaker.

"Looks like you've been working out," I say. "But it won't be enough for you to beat me. You sit on your ass too much in an office."

Behind his fists, Darius has his chin up. He looks ridiculous, like a Victorian boxer about to engage in fisticuffs. "Like you've been keeping yourself in top form. When was the last time you had a mission?"

I don't answer.

"Matthias says you're turning into a hermit." Darius continues circling me. "Completely checked out of the family. What's the point of you living here if you're not going to help us?"

"Us? You left the mountain." I throw a few test punches, but they're half-hearted and Darius knows it. He doesn't even dodge. That's the one downside of fighting a twin. Sometimes he knows my own mind better than I know it myself.

Or maybe his plan is to talk me to death.

"Who do you think pays the bills?" Darius rants. "Who paid for Matthias to go through med school? Who got the grant to install the new solar panels Everest wanted? Who do you think does Ma's taxes? You think I went to business school for fun?"

"Yeah. Fun and profit. You'd do anything for a buck." I jab and jab, but Darius surprises me by ducking and darting past me, his fist catching me in the kidney as he goes.

I'm breathing hard when we face off again. "You broke Ma's heart."

"You broke it first."

He's not wrong. Maybe this fight is just a way of punishing myself. When I felt like I needed a licking, Darius was always good for it.

So be it. I wade in for more penance, ducking his fist and tackling him. We end up on the ground—him punching my head, me trying to crush his ribs.

A growl shakes the ground. I don't know if the sound comes from my throat or his.

"No animals," I grunt. "The human."

"So you haven't told her yet."

"That info's on a need-to-know basis. You know how it is." I don't add that Lana may have found out I'm a shifter. Darius doesn't need another reason to ride my ass.

We're face to face now, kicking up dust. Our fight has turned into a floor wrestling match.

Darius blinks through dirt-covered lashes at me. "What I don't get is why you chose another human. Wasn't Tiffany bad enough?"

Even here, on the ground, grappling with my brother, Lana's honeyed scent fills my nostrils. "She's not mine."

"Oh." Darius cranes his head. "She's gorgeous. Maybe I'll give her a ride in my helicopter after—"

With a yell, I scissor my legs, gaining momentum to scrabble upwards and get my hands around my twin's throat. I really am going to kill him this time.

LANA

A cloud of dust covers Teddy and Darius. Growls and snarls escape, but I can't make out what's happening. All the dirt flying around turns the two fighters into amorphous shadow monsters writhing on the ground.

"Can't you stop them?" I cry to Matthias.

He shrugs. "It's best to let them fight it out."

"Matthias!"

"You want me to get pummeled too?"

A roar rings out, and the few birds who'd returned to the trees after the helicopter left take flight.

"You need to get inside." Matthias tries to herd me back. I pretend to obey then dash around him.

"Teddy! Help!"

"Lana?" A figure rises from the dust. Teddy lowers his fists, his full focus on me.

All my breath escapes my lungs. Teddy was in full fight mode, and he stopped. For me.

Unfortunately Darius doesn't get the message that Teddy's declared a ceasefire. He whales on Teddy a few more times before he realizes brother's just standing there.

Teddy glares at him, spits blood, and shoulders him out of the way to stride to me.

"You okay?" His knuckles are swollen from pummeling his brother, but his fingers are gentle as he cups my face.

"I think I might faint," I say in a small voice. It's true. That fight was something else. I'm wheezing on all the dust and pollen they kicked up.

"Lana needs quiet and rest," Matthias says. "This is not helping."

Darius' nice suit is dirty. His shirt gapes open, missing a few buttons. But he looks pretty decent for a guy who got punched a few times in the face. There's a faint mottling of purple shadows around his eye and jaw, but other than these bruises, he looks unharmed.

Teddy has blood trickling down from a cut over his eye. "Show's over." He lifts me in his burly arms and carries me toward the cabin. I flail a second before snuggling close. Teddy's body temperature is running hot. I duck my head and sniff his neck. Mmmm, manly sweat.

He must look like the conquering hero carrying off the girl. The way he takes charge makes my panties wet.

"Good fight, brother," Darius calls.

Teddy stops on the stoop. "It was a good fight. You did good for a suit," he says to his twin.

Darius raises his chin. "I found some sparring buddies. A friend named Brick Blackthroat owns a private sport club for…fighters like us."

Teddy grunts and turns his back on his brother. "Get out of here," he calls over his shoulder. "You're not welcome anymore." He kicks the cabin door shut. It slams behind us, and I squeak.

"Sorry." Teddy marches us to the couch and sets me down. His shoulders are bunched, his muscles tense like he's about to storm back out of the cabin and put his brother in a coffin. And I can't have that.

He grunts when I put a hand on his chest. His white t-shirt is stained with more than dirt. There's a reddish brown smear I'm pretty sure is blood.

"You're hurt." I rise to my knees and, without stopping to think, pull up his shirt. I freeze as I get a faceful of the most epically muscled chest I've ever seen. It's dust-streaked and dirty but beautiful.

"Lana," Teddy says, and I realize he's been saying my name for a while.

I could spend an eternity staring at the perfect planes

and grooves of his abs and chest, but there's a nasty bruise on his right pec and another down by his side. "He got you good. I can call Matthias—"

"No." Teddy rumbles. "Give me a moment, babygirl." He drops to the coffee table and rubs a hand over his face.

"You look stressed. C'mere, I'll rub your shoulders." I reach up and dig my thumbs into the rigid swell of muscle beside his neck, babbling. "Yikes, yes, your muscles are like boulders."

His face is still hidden behind his hand. "This is a bad idea."

Crap, he doesn't want to flirt. "I'm sorry." I snatch my hands back. "If you're not interested—"

"Not interested?" He glowers at me and puts my hand right on the front of his jeans. His cock prods my palm. "I'm interested, babygirl." He breathes in my ear. "I'm two seconds away from ripping off your pretty pink outfit and seeing how sweet your pussy tastes."

I let out a half squeak, half whimper.

He leans over me. His head drops to the curve of my neck. My spine loosens, and my insides heat. The pine-scented air of the cabin is too thick to breathe.

"Teddy—"

"Shhhh." He nuzzles my jaw, rubbing my soft cheek with his blond scruff. I'm swooning in the scent of him when he mutters, "Fuck it." He turns his head and takes my mouth with his.

Teddy tastes like mint and honey. I arch into him as he cups the back of my neck, holding me still for his plunder. My breasts are swollen, my nipples are tight and threatening to cut through the reinforced shelf bra in my camisole. It's too much. It's not enough. I need more.

He shoves down my camisole and sucks on one eager nipple then the other. I grind my clit down on his massive dick. I surge up right at the same time he pushes closer. The move knocks our heads together, and I groan.

Dang it!

"Shit, Lana. You're still hurt." He pulls away and tugs his shirt down.

"Me? I'm fine. What about you? He got you a few times." His cut isn't bleeding any more, but there's still that bruise. Covering it with a t-shirt isn't going to make me forget it. "Do you need Matthias to check you out?"

"No. I'll just be a minute. Gonna clean up." He bounds up and disappears into the bedroom.

I bite my lip. I guess badass mountain men tape themselves up after a fight.

The front door opens and Matthias strolls in. His doctor's bag is a bit dusty from the showdown in front of the cabin, but he's smiling. "How's Teddy?"

"He says he's fine."

Matthias chuckles at my doubtful tone. "As long as he's up and breathing without wheezing, he'll be all right."

Geez. How bad do these brother fights get?

"It's okay, Lana." Matthias reads my face all too well. "Barely a day goes by without one of my brothers punching another for no good reason."

"I see. Good thing you're a doctor."

"Yeah, good thing. I'm going to head out, follow Darius, make sure he gets off the mountain. You need to take it easy." He picks up the bag of frozen blueberries, wipes off the condensation and hands it to me.

"Yes, Doctor." I put the bag to my head, wincing at the cold. I can hear Teddy moving around the bedroom behind the shut door, so I add, in a whisper, "I take it Darius doesn't visit often?"

"Not Teddy. I keep in touch with him. He did pay for my medical schooling."

There are so many questions I want to ask. "Will he be okay? He sent his ride away."

"There's a helicopter pad nearby. He can pick up a ride there. Or one of our brothers can give him a ride. Axel's headed down the mountain. Have you met Axel yet?"

I shake my head. "You and Darius are the only brothers I've met. I would remember someone named Axel."

"I'm sure you'll meet the whole crew before long. Teddy is our big brother. Everyone looks up to him."

I try to sort through all the accusations Teddy and Darius threw at each other, but it's too much. I hug my knees to my chest. "Maybe I shouldn't stay here. I could go. I'm in the way."

"No," Teddy barks from the bedroom.

"You're not in the way," Matthias soothes.

"Okay." I can stay here for at least one night. I let my head fall back against the couch cushions. "But after all that excitement, I need to lie down."

"Rest," Matthias commands and nods to Teddy before leaving and gently closing the cabin door.

Teddy paces towards me. He cleaned up and changed into a new white t-shirt–identical to the one he was wearing before. The cut on his face is healing fast. The skin was split before he went into the bedroom but not now. His head is down, and he seems to be studying his bare feet. He fought barefoot against his brother. Wild man.

"I'm sorry you had to see that," Teddy mutters.

"Oh no, it was interesting. I learned a lot."

Teddy raises a brow.

"No, seriously, it was a masterclass in how to piss you off." I hold up a finger. "First step, use your full name." Teddy doesn't laugh, so I try a new tack. "It's okay. That's how family is, right? Siblings hold the nuclear codes to your temper. They know just what buttons to push."

"Still. It was ugly, and I didn't want you to see it."

"I'm okay. Thank you for defending me." At least, I think he was defending me. I want to know more about Tiffany and about Darius, but they're obviously sensitive subjects. "Do you fight like that with all your brothers?"

"All the time."

My eyes widen. "Even Matthias?"

"Matthias brawls as much as the rest of us. He's just smarter about it. With him, the fight's over almost as soon as it starts."

"Twins and triplets. My God. Your poor mother.

"Trust me, she could handle us."

"Could?" I gulp. Has Teddy been referring to his mother in the past tense, and I missed it? Did she die?

"She's not dead. She's just…taking some time to herself."

"Does she live close?"

"We all live on the mountain."

"You and all your brothers? Or…almost all of them," I backtrack when I remember Darius. "Do all your brothers have cute cabins like this one? Are the triplets identical too? When can I meet them?"

"Yes, no, and never." He straightens with a frown.

6

Lana

"You sure you're feeling better?" Teddy asks as he serves me pancakes on the couch.

"Great. Much better. I probably shouldn't do any jumping jacks today, but I avoid doing jumping jacks even when I don't have a head injury. My boobs once snapped a sports bra after only three jumps."

Teddy blinks and holds my gaze in a masterful attempt not to glance down at my boobs. "Have you remembered anything else from yesterday?"

"No, I don't think so. But if I rest up, I bet I'll be remembering everything in no time. I just need a little peace and quiet."

"Okay, babygirl. Peace and quiet I can do."

A blast of sound blows the door open. I shriek and throw up my hands to cover my ears, forgetting I'm holding a fork. It goes flying. Teddy shoves off the couch so fast it nearly topples over with me in it. He stomps to the door, shouting something I can't hear him over the din. Whatever's making the noise outside, it sounds like a million weasels getting crushed by a church organ. It's so loud and so bad, my eyes water.

A second after Teddy exits the cabin, the noise falls away, leaving blissful silence. I wipe tears from my eyes and head outside to see what's up.

Teddy stands on the stoop, facing three shaggy haired young men. The first and third are in matching plaid kilts. The first is shirtless, showing a scrawny white chest. The one in the middle is dressed head-to-toe in black, and behind the screen of hair in his face, his eyes are rimmed with guyliner.

They're all holding red plaid bladders studded with ornate black reeds. Bagpipes. That explains the noise.

The shirtless one tosses his hair out of his face, angles his head, and blows a blasting note on his instrument. The sound is like needles in my head.

"No," shouts Teddy, and the teen drops the instrument.

"C'mon, big bro. If we don't practice, how are we supposed to get paying gigs?"

Teddy folds his burly arms over his chest. "You think people are lining up to pay someone to play the bagpipes?"

"No," he scoffs. "The plan is to show up and play, so people will pay for us to go away."

The young man all in black tilts his head, causing more of his hair to fall in his face. "Then why do we need to practice? Won't it work better if we suck?"

"Enough," Teddy barks. "We're not practicing today. We're not forming a bagpipe band."

"Fine." The shirtless guy says. "I have plenty more ideas."

"Hey," the third perks up. "Do I smell pancakes?"

"No," Teddy says, but I push out the door to stand beside him.

"Yes," I correct. "We have plenty. I'm not going to eat five pounds of bacon."

"Bacon?" the shirtless one says hopefully.

The other two stare at me. Their shoulder-length hair is still in their faces, but I can see enough of them to tell they're identical.

"OMG!" I say. "You must be the triplets."

"The Terrible Threes," Teddy murmurs under his breath. I poke him in the side.

"Who are you?" the kid in black asks.

"I'm Lana." I look expectantly at Teddy until he sighs and makes introductions.

"Hutch, Bern, and Canyon." He points to each in turn. "You can come inside and eat pancakes. But no bothering my guest. And no bagpipes." He glares at Hutch, whose bagpipe just let out a muffled squeak.

"Fine." The goth looking one, Bern, drops his bagpipe to the ground. The other two fall in line. They file in after Teddy. The shirtless one, Canyon, winks at me.

Once in the cabin, they fall into a practiced routine. Bern and Canyon flick their hair out of their face long enough to unpin a long pine plank from the wall and set it up as a table. They disappear out the door and return with five polished stumps to use as seats. Teddy mans the stove, sliding trays of bacon into the oven and making stacks of small, sand-dollar sized pancakes, while Hutch sets the table and ferries food too and fro.

I sit on the couch and watch the activity until Canyon invites me to join them. He puts my plate at one end of the plank, and replaces my fallen fork with a new one as smoothly as a waiter at a restaurant. The cabin feels much smaller with three new guys in it, even if the guys are gangly teens moving in a synchronized breakfast dance.

But judging by the amount of pancakes they cram into their mouths, they'll be filling out with muscle soon.

"So, Lana," Canyon, the flirty, shirtless triplet, scoots his stump closer to me. "How do you know Teddy?"

I give him a gentle smile, trying to give off mom or older sister vibes, so this young man doesn't think I'm flirting. "We just met. I was hiking, and I fell and hit my head, and he rescued me."

"She spent the night here." Teddy leans over me to put a fresh stack of pancakes on my plate.

"And now, he says I'm his prisoner." I poke his side as he passes. He tweaks my braid, then straightens and shoots a stern look at his flirtatious brother.

Canyon clears his throat. "So you just met yesterday?"

I shrug. "I figured no one named Teddy can be a serial killer."

Bern raises his head. "What about Ted Bundy?"

I flounder for a second before amending, "No one named Teddy, who also has a bedroom decorated with cute bears, is a serial killer."

The triplets nod as if this is logical. Teddy rolls his eyes. "Eat," he orders me.

"Yes sir," I snark back.

Canyon turns to his fellow triplets. "So the bagpipe band is out. New plan. We join the Army."

Teddy slams the oven shut. "Absolutely not."

"You joined the Army when you were our age," Canyon points out.

I perk up at this. I could scarf facts about Teddy like sand dollar pancakes. "How old are you guys?"

"Eighteen," Hutch says proudly.

Yikes. They seem so young. I turn to Teddy. "You joined the Army when you were eighteen?"

"Yeah. I was a kid. It broke Ma's heart."

I swallow, remembering Darius and Teddy's fight. *"You broke Ma's heart."* Teddy accused Darius, who retorted, *"You broke it first."*

"Ma wanted me to go to college, but it didn't work out."

"Teddy was in the special forces," Canyon tells me. "Hutch thinks we can get recruited by his commander. Beat all Teddy's records."

Teddy slams a serving plate stacked with bacon down in the center of the table and points a finger at each of the Terrible Threes. "No Army."

"But the signing bonus—"

"No. We'll find another way."

I must look puzzled because Canyon leans close. "We need money."

"Money?" I perk up. "I love money. I can help. I run my own company."

"Wait," Hutch snaps his fingers. "I know you. You're Lana. You're famous."

Teddy's brows snap together. "What?"

"What?" the other two of the Terrible Threes echo.

"I've seen you on Insta. You model for GoddessWear."

"Yeah," I say. "In the beginning, I couldn't afford models, so I did it myself. I still do the occasional promotion."

"Wait, you own that company?" Hutch asks.

I shrug. "I do. I started it instead of going to college. I used to sew all my own outfits in high school."

"Cute clothes for curvy girls," Hutch repeats my company's tagline, and I beam.

"That's right! This is from my new hiking line." I rise and point my toe to show off my lightweight pants.

"Very nice." Hutch scoots his stump to look closer. "Great stitching. Is it cut on a bias?"

"Why, yes! Do you sew?"

"Ma made us learn," Bern, the goth teen, says through a curtain of his hair. "Hutch is the best at it."

Hutch points to Teddy's bedroom. "I made those curtains."

"OMG!" I squeal. "I love those curtains. I'm thinking of doing something with cute little bears for my winter line."

"OMG!" echoes Hutch with similar enthusiasm.

"There are bears everywhere here," I say. "I've already seen three. It's been amazing."

"Yeah, we've got lots of bears." Hutch laughs nervously.

"Do you see them too? One of them came right into the cabin and opened the fridge."

"Um, no, that's never happened to me." His gaze darts around like crazy. The other two triplets stare at their plates.

"I'm thinking of doing a photoshoot here. Get some sexy mountain men to model for us. Who knows, maybe we'll get a shot or two of the bears!"

A frozen silence sweeps the room. Hutch's Adam's apple bobs up and down. "I'm not sure that's a good idea…"

"Why not?"

Teddy pushes away from the table. "Lana, you'll have to excuse us. I need to talk to my brothers. Outside."

∽

Teddy

I stalk to the edge of the meadow, towards the treeline separating my cabin from the beehives, with my brothers pinging me with questions.

"What's going on?" Hutch asks.

"Are you and Lana dating? And is she serious about the photoshoot?" Canyon flexes his skinny torso. "I could model."

"Does she know about us?" This, quietly, from Bern.

I whirl on them, and they fall silent. "No modeling. And, as for whether or not she knows what we are...I don't know. She might have seen me turn, but she hit her head, and there are blanks in her memory. I'm trying to figure out what she knows."

"You could seduce her," Canyon waggles his brows. "Get her to tell you."

"We're not dating." *Mate*, my bear reminds me. I gnash my teeth. "Is she really famous?"

"Uh, yeah." Hutch digs for his phone. He clicks around and presents the screen to me. In the photograph, Lana smiles sleepily at the camera, her hair styled in a soft fro. A yellow bikini caresses her curves, and her brown cheeks have a subtle glow that mimics the flush of an orgasm.

Mine, my bear growls.

"Geez, Teddy, don't grip it so tight." Hutch tries to grab his phone back, and I hold him off. "You're gonna break it!"

I'm breathing hard. "Can you delete this?"

"No, it's on Instagram. There are a whole bunch of them, see?" He scrolls through the feed, and my body temperature must hit 103 degrees. There's Lana in jeans and a flirty little white off-the-shoulder top, perched on a Corvette. Lana as a pinup-girl, with bouncing curls and scarlett lips to match her tight red dress. She looks incredible. My dick pulses in my jeans. I'm probably one in a million men who are jacking off to this bombshell.

Hutch won't meet my eyes. "If you downloaded any

photos of her, delete them. Now." I shove the phone back into his hands.

"So you *are* screwing her," Canyon says. "Or you want to."

"No. It's...complicated."

Bern bows his head, so his hair falls in his face. "So it's like Tiffany all over again."

"No," I growl. "It's not going to be like that."

"Are you going to tell Lana about us?" Hutch asks. "About what we are?"

"She might already know. She saw Everest taking care of the bees. And yesterday she saw Axel raiding my freezer."

"Oh yeah," Canyon says. "Axel told us. He says he just wanted the deer sausage—"

"He has his own fridge," I say. "I don't know why he puts stuff in mine."

"The same reason we put the chickens by you," Hutch says. "And why Everest keeps the hives over here. We're keeping an eye on you, for Ma. She's worried."

I throw up my hands. "Ma's asleep!"

"Well, she would be worried, if she wasn't hibernating. Matthias said it was good for us to check on you."

"Matthias doesn't know what's best for everyone," I snap. "New rule. No one comes over here unless they're in human form. Tell Axel and Everest."

"But Everest has to check the bees," Hutch says. "You know he likes to do it in bear form. He says they don't sting him as much."

"Tell him to wear the beekeeper's suit."

"He hates the beekeeper's suit."

I pinch the bridge of my nose. "Fine. I'll deal with it."

Canyon steps into my space. "What are you going to do about Lana?"

Tie her to the bed and claim her, my bear suggests. "I don't know yet."

"You're not going to mindwipe her, are you?" Canyon glowers.

No! My bear shouts so loud, I'm surprised everyone can't hear him. "If she knows what we are, that's exactly what I have to do."

"But it's not fair," Hutch sidles next to Canyon. Now there's a wall of three scrawny brothers blocking me from returning to the cabin. "She wouldn't tell anyone."

"You don't know that."

"She won't. You can trust her. She's not Tiffany," Bern says, and I whirl on him, ready to throw a punch.

Three identical faces glare up at me.

I marshall my temper. These are my little brothers, and they mean well. "Look, I have to mindwipe her. She may have seen me turn. She hit her head and doesn't remember."

The Terrible Threes wilt. "When are you going to do it?" Canyon asks.

"Soon. I'm waiting to make sure her head heals, so it doesn't mess her up more than it already will." I'm fooling myself. Getting memories wiped will affect any human. I can only hope it doesn't alter her too much.

Bern shakes his head. Hutch looks like I ate his pet hamster.

"It's wrong," Canyon says, his hands bunched into fists. "Can't you just—"

"There's no other way." I need to shut this down. Now. "We can't trust humans. You know that. And family comes first." I push past the line of my brothers and head towards the cabin. "I'll tell Lana you said goodbye."

7

Teddy

When I get back to the cabin, the shower is running. I shuffle around the kitchen, cleaning up.

It's now or never. I should call Matthias to call a car and take Lana to the nearest leech. If she protests or struggles, we'll have to sedate her. That's what we had to do with Tiffany.

The thought of treating Lana like that makes my stomach churn. But I can't risk letting her off this mountain without being sure she doesn't know our secret, and I can't keep her here forever.

Then there's the matter of her step-brother. Once Rafe finds him, I'll need to figure out if he's still a threat to Lana.

If he is, he won't be for long. I will end him.

"Teddy?" she calls from the bathroom, and I race across the room, using shifter speed to get to her side.

At the last second, I stop short in the bedroom. Dammit, not again. I can't keep slipping. It's like my bear wants Lana to know what I really am.

The bathroom door is cracked open, but I rap on it anyway. "What is it? Are you all right? Are you hurt?"

"No, I'm good. Come in." She greets me with a smile that slams into my gut like a fist. She's so beautiful. So sunny. I've known her less than a day, and I can't imagine not having her in my life.

"Look at this." She points to her forehead. She's removed the bandage, and the skin underneath is smooth and unscarred.

The serum Matthias used worked too well. I am going to have to mindwipe her.

"The cut is totally healed! Isn't it weird and wonderful?"

"Yeah," I mumble, sagging in the doorway.

"It didn't even leave a scar." She leans into the mirror, examining her head this way and that. "And my head is a lot better, too. I feel better than I have in a long time, actually. Must be all the fresh mountain air."

"Must be."

She turns and looks up at me through her lashes, and I realize two things. One, she's wearing only a towel. Two, the way she bites her lip makes me want to take a bite out of her.

"Teddy? Did you hear me?"

"Hmm?"

"I said I need to get my phone working. Touch base with my company, check my Instagram. I haven't been off social media this long since the summer my nanny took my phone away for flunking French."

No. I can't let her get a working phone. I can't let her go. "You didn't tell me you owned a company," I stall.

"It didn't come up. It's nice to be off the grid like this." She sweeps her braids back, baring her shoulders. The towel is slipping, showing off sweet curves of her breast.

I step closer, needing to be near her. "So it's true. You are famous."

She shrugs, and the towel inches lower. "A little."

Shit. All the more reason to mindwipe her. She could make one phone call and be in front of cameras, telling the world about shifters.

She's not Tiffany.

"Teddy? Are you okay?"

My voice is husky. "I'm fine, babygirl." One of her braids is askew, so I brush it straight. Her honeyed scent fills the room.

"It was great meeting the triplets," she says. "They seem so young, though."

"Yeah. They've been a bit sheltered. They were homeschooled. If they come off as immature, that's why."

"I think they are sweet." She leans into me, almost unconsciously. "You've been so great. Rescuing me, taking care of me. I'm really grateful. But I don't need any more rest. It's been fun being your prisoner, but I really don't have a reason to stay." She bites one plush lip. "Unless… you give me one."

I toy with one of her braids.

She closes her hand over mine. "So that settles it? I should go?"

"No." I fist my hand in her braids and gently pull her head back.

"Teddy?" Her lips part, and I can't take it anymore. I tilt my head and kiss her.

∼

Lana

Teddy leans over me, holding me upright with his hand in my hair. His mouth slants over mine, taking, plundering.

"You're not leaving," he growls, and the sound vibrates through me, making me shudder. I let the towel drop.

He hoists me up and lays me out on the bed, covering his body with mine. "All night, I was dying to do this."

Squee!

He rears up between my legs and cups my pussy, grinding down with his palm.

"Does it ache right here, babygirl? Do you want me to make it better?"

"Yes, please." My hips are already rocking. He brushes a finger against my entrance, and I shoot up off the bed.

"Easy," he murmurs.

"What about you?" I put my hand to his crotch. There's a throbbing monster hiding in his jeans, and I can't wait to meet it. "This feels hard and painful. I can kiss it better…"

"Later." His fingers probe my entrance. "I'm going to be gentle, baby. This time."

"You don't have to be."

"Don't tempt me." He nuzzles my belly, finding a few stretch marks and kisses them. My breath catches in my throat.

He continues licking and kissing his way down, his beard teasing my soft flesh. I writhe, ticklish, and he slides his big hands up the back of my legs, hooking behind my knees and holding me open.

"Yes, babygirl," he breathes, drinking in the sight of my splayed pussy. "This is what I want."

The first soft kiss on my mons sends ripples of pleasure through me. I reach down and grab Teddy's head. He captures my wrists and pins them to my side.

"Be good," he orders, "or I'll tie you to the bed."

"OMG," I pant.

I try to be good, but after a few more kisses, I'm

squirming too much for Teddy's liking. He rises up and rolls me over, delivering three sharp swats to my ass. I moan and arch my back. If I'm bad at being good, I'll be good at being bad.

"That's it, babygirl." His beard tickles my bottom as he kisses each cheek. I wriggle some more, on purpose, and earn another round of sexy spanking.

The bears aren't the only ones who are naughty on this mountain.

"So much for gentle. Is that all you got?" I press my front into the bed and bounce my butt higher. His palm sears me, but the pain morphs into something else, something wonderful. I feel the shock of sensation right in my pussy. "Yes, like that. Harder."

"How is it you're so perfect for me?" he mutters, and I melt into a puddle of happiness. "C'mere."

He tugs me up and positions me on my knees, facing the headboard. He lies down and guides me to straddle him. I grab the headboard and rise up as Teddy palms my ass, pulling my pussy up to his face.

"I need to taste you," he growls. "Give it to me."

"I don't know." He tries to tug me down, but I resist. "I'll suffocate you."

"I'll die happy."

I lower myself and let my pussy make full contact with his face. He nuzzles into me. "Hang onto the headboard."

I hang onto the headboard for dear life. His tongue dips and swirls into my folds. I dig my nails into the pine and angle my hips, rocking over his mouth. His tongue catches my clit, and I shudder, lifting off him for a moment. I can't move very far because his fingers grip my ass, keeping me close.

"That's it, babygirl," comes his muffled voice. "Grind down. Let me give you what you need."

I give into gravity and Teddy's inexorable pull, and let my weight sink down again. His beard tickles the tender skin of my inner thighs. His tongue is everywhere, snaking into my entrance, swirling around my clit, sucking up my juices like its ambrosia. Like he can't get enough.

His strong lips and probing tongue combine with the soft tickling of his beard, sending pleasure slamming into me. "Oh my God," I gasp, and fall sideways onto the bed. He rolls with me, his face still between my legs. He nibbles my labia, gives my clit a kiss, and sits up, licking his lips. He rests a large hand between my legs, pressing his thick long finger in me lightly to ground me. It takes forever for my orgasm's aftershocks to subside.

"That was just the beginning," Teddy promises, wiping the wetness from his beard.

"My turn," I declare.

Teddy's groan sounds pained. His eyes have more than darkened. They almost look like they changed color–from grey to a warm, honey brown. "Let me just get inside you." His voice is gruff and thick. He rips his shirt off over his head and unbuttons his jeans. "Would that be okay?"

Um, yes please. I clear my throat and say what I want. "I'm on birth control and I'm clean."

"I'm clean," he says. "We can use protection if you want, but I don't have any STDs."

"I trust you."

Those words seem to do something to Teddy. His eyes flash even darker, and a strange growl comes from his throat.

"You sound like one of the bad bears." I help him shove his jeans down his hips.

He steps off the bed to shuck them. "This bad bear needs you right now. Desperately."

"I need you, too," I tell him. It's true. Having his

mouth on me was amazing, but there's something about the completion of penetration that I crave. That biological urge to engage in the act that actually produces babies. Not that we're going to do that.

Except the idea of carrying Teddy's baby suddenly takes hold in my mind with huge appeal. He's such a giver. He'd be a rock during a pregnancy. I'd bet my life on it. I'm suddenly furiously jealous of the hypothetical mother of his child.

He climbs over me, stopping to kiss and lick between my legs, then traveling upward, dragging his open mouth across my thick belly, then taking one hard, brown nipple between his lips.

I arch and cry out the moment he sucks it, the answering tug going directly to my core.

"I need you," I repeat, reaching for his cock. I find it and fist the base, making him growl again as it jerks and lengthens in my hand. I love that he growls. Such a perfect mountain man.

His cock is thick and hard, longer than I've ever seen—even on porn. "I need to give it to you," he answers, rising up over me and letting me guide him to my entrance.

"Yes, please."

"Aw, babygirl. I was trying to be gentle. But you're driving me out of my mind." He spears me with one powerful stroke, and I gasp at the deep penetration.

"Oh God!"

He goes still, his fingers sweeping my braids from my face. "You okay, babygirl? Too much?"

I shake my head, my body already accommodating his size. "No, it's perfect. Give it to me."

"Fuck," he mutters. His hips snap as he drives up into me.

I'm not small or light, but he uses enough force to send

me sliding up the mattress toward the headboard. He catches me where neck meets shoulder and holds me in place for his pounding.

He's rough.

Passionate.

Very, very hard.

And I can't get enough of it. Each slam into me seems to affirm something about me I didn't know I was missing.

The sense of being wanted.

I'm not sure I realized until now how unwanted I really felt. By my parents, by Bentley. I never fit in. Not in my family. Not in my community. Growing up, no one knew what to do with me—a rich black girl in Los Angeles, the stepdaughter of a director.

Teddy knows, though.

Teddy knows exactly what to do to me. With me. For me.

He pounds into me like our lives depend on it. Like this is as life-affirming and soul-fulfilling for him as it is for me.

I rock my hips to meet him, to take him deeper. I squeeze my internal muscles around his cock to give him more sensation, and he lets out an unearthly growl. Truly, a strange sound that seems to shake the cabin.

"Yes!" I shout, as if that sound is as familiar as my own name even though I've never heard those notes before in my life.

He growls again.

I reach up and pinch his flat nipple, and he goes wild, thrashing his head, slamming in with such force my eyes roll back in my head.

The moment he comes, I let go, coming with him, my muscles squeezing and milking his cock. I swear I feel his cum inside me, searing me with heat, christening me with love.

Teddy drops his head to my neck, and I feel the scrape of something sharp, and then he jerks his torso roughly back, covering his mouth with his hand.

I'm too out of my mind to comprehend what's happening. Maybe he gets embarrassed about his orgasm face.

The thought makes me laugh, and I wrap my legs behind his back and pull him down to me again in a fit of giggles.

"Lana," he pants. "Oh Fate. You're going to be the death of me."

~

Teddy

I ALMOST MARKED HER.

Holy hell—my bear is completely out of control. I had no idea I was going to do that. I push away all the implications of my bear marking a human female.

I can't think about that now.

When we've caught our breaths and she's stopped laughing, I ease out of her.

"I need a moment." I head out to grab her a glass of water and halt in the living room. My front door is askew. There are no bears in my kitchen, and nothing on the kitchen counters or in the living room has moved, but there's a piece of paper under a rock on the breakfast table. The corner of the note flaps in the breeze from the open front door.

"Hey, big bro, thanks for breakfast. We borrowed the warbird for an errand, but we'll bring it back by tonight. xoxo, TTT."

TTT stands for "The Terrible Threes". It's how the

triplets sign their handiwork. The little buggers must have snuck in while I was with Lana.

The hidden key rack in my kitchen cupboard is missing the helicopter keys.

"Goddammit," I snarl. They could've stolen the keys while I was with Lana or earlier when they were helping me with breakfast.

I've taken my brothers up in my helicopter before. They've done parachute jumps, and I've even started teaching them how to fly. Bern shows the most aptitude, but he's not cleared for solo flights. Not by a long shot.

If they wreck my warbird, they better hope they die in the crash. I will make them wish they were dead.

"Is everything all right?" Lana calls. She's still in bed, her eyes sleepy. I shove on my boots and lope to her side to lean down for a kiss.

"It's all good, babygirl. There's a…family emergency. I need to take care of it, but I'll be right back."

Her forehead wrinkles, and she sits up. "Do you want me to—"

"No. Stay. I mean it. I want you here—in this bed—when I return."

"Okay." She relaxes back with a sigh. "I might take a little nap. Get ready for round two."

My cock throbs, and I almost crawl back in bed to take her in my arms again. Claim her properly.

Instead, I have to go out and save the Terrible Threes from themselves.

˜

LANA

I'm lying in a sex haze on the bed, contemplating the

beard burn on the inside of my thighs, when someone raps on the window.

"Lana?"

I roll, making sure I'm swathed in the blanket comforter. "Who is it?" I peer through the curtains just as one of the Terrible Threes presses his face to the glass. No way for me to tell which triplet he is. He's not wearing guyliner, and he has a shirt on, so my best guess is this is Hutch.

"It's Hutch," he confirms in a whisper. "I'm here to rescue you."

"What?"

"Quick, get dressed." He points to my pile of clothes and ducks away.

I scramble to do as he says, pulling everything on in record time. He meets me in the living room.

"Is everything okay?" I ask. For some reason, I'm also whispering.

"Everything's fine. Let's go. Where are your shoes?" He fetches them and holds them close, so I can cram my feet into them. "Is this everything?" He darts into the bedroom to grab my pink pack. "Come on. We got to move."

"What? Where's Teddy?"

"He's busy. We distracted him, but it won't last long."

"What are you talking about?"

"Quick, before he comes back." He seizes my hand and drags me out of the cabin.

"Hutch, stop." I stagger to keep up with him. "What is going on? Why are we rushing?"

Halfway across the meadow, a loud whoop makes me look up. A helicopter sails overhead, with a shirtless teen shouting, "Yeehaw!" as he hangs from the skids.

I stop and gape, even as Hutch pushes me along. "Was that Canyon?"

"Yep. He and Bern stole Teddy's warbird to distract him, so you can escape."

Escape?

"Hutch, I know I joked about being Teddy's prisoner, but I was just kidding…"

Hutch tugs me into the forest. "Please, Lana, trust me. You have to get out now."

"Okay," I soothe. He seems super intent on 'rescuing me'. I have no idea what Hutch is up to, but it won't hurt to go with the flow. I'll go with him and see if I can get my phone fixed or charged. Check in with my company. Maybe hit a store for some fresh clothes, so I can stay longer with Teddy. "Can I at least leave a note or something for Teddy?"

"I'll tell him you'll be right back." Hutch marches me past the beehives. "Here. I have to go back. Follow the trail down to the creek. My brother Everest is meeting you there. He found your rental car."

I perk up. I'd forgotten about the rental car. "He did?"

"Yeah, this morning. He'll take you to it. You have the keys?"

"I think so…" I dig in my pink pack. Now that I've remembered the car, I remember how Bentley fussed at me to make sure I didn't "do something dumb" and lose the car keys. "I put them in the special inner pocket. Here." I hold them up, and Hutch nods.

"Good. Follow the trail." He points to the worn path between the trees. "Everest will meet you at the creek."

"Okay." I want to ask how I'll recognize Everest, but Hutch is already hurrying away. I shoulder my pack and hike down. I'm already making plans about what to tell my team, so I can extend my vacation. Maybe tonight I can seduce Teddy in the bath…and in the morning, make him breakfast in bed.

I guess I should try to find out what happened to Bentley. Teddy said he has a team of people trying to find him, but I can't imagine why they haven't located him yet. It doesn't make sense. For some reason, I don't feel like he's lost and alone on the mountain. My gut tells me he left me and hiked down the mountain. Of course, he didn't have the keys to the car–but he's the type who could just hire his way out of any situation.

Once I get my phone working, I can try calling him.

I stride down the trail, humming to myself, never noticing the silent shadow gliding alongside.

∼

Teddy

I steam up the mountain towards the cabin.

Hutch is waiting for me on the stoop. "Don't be mad." He rises with his hands up in the universal gesture of surrender.

"Too late," I snap. "I spent a half hour chasing down your idiot brothers."

"Are they okay?"

"They nearly crashed the bird." I shoulder past him and take in the quiet cabin. My bedroom door creaks open. The bed is empty. I whirl on Hutch.

"Where's Lana?"

His Adam's apple bobs. "Gone."

"What?"

He straightens. "I couldn't let you mindwipe her."

I sputter, but my phone buzzes. Only a few people have my number, and they don't call unless it's urgent. "Don't move," I order Hutch and take the call.

"Teddy," It's Rafe. "We got a hit on that guy you wanted tracked. Bentley Dupree."

"Yeah?"

"It's bad, brother. He put out a hit on your girl, Lana Langmeyer. Ten million to take her out."

The whole world slows to a stop. Ten million is enough to tempt an assassin. For that amount, Bentley could hire the best of the best. A whole team of assassins.

"Tell me the job's still open," I say.

"I wish I could. It looks like someone took it. You need to get Lana to a safe place, stat."

I hang up and turn to Hutch. His face is white.

"Did you hear that?"

He nods.

"Someone's trying to kill Lana. We need to find her. Now."

∽

LANA

I hear the creek before I see it. It's up ahead, glinting through the creosote, but there's no sign of anyone waiting for me. Not a burly mountain man or a respectable looking doctor or an identical triplet. What will Everest look like?

A giant shadow moves between the trees, and I whirl, hugging my bag to my chest. "Everest?"

A long furry head with a black snout emerges from between two aspen trees. I freeze, face to face with the biggest bear I've ever seen. It looks familiar. Slowly, it moves into a patch of sunlight, and its white fur shows up clearly.

Oh my God. It's the same bear that was at the beehives. I couldn't see its fur then, but I can now. It's a yellowy white, head to toe. A polar bear. Not a pizzly bear.

It rises to hind legs, and I gape up at it. It beckons with a paw.

Is this for real?

I look around but there's no sign of Hutch's brother, Everest. Instead, there's a huge polar bear snuffing impatiently and jerking his head as if indicating to me to follow it. It drops to all fours and trots down the trail, then moves like it's beckoning me with that big paw again.

Alrighty then. I nod and follow the polar bear's lumbering form through a pine grove.

It takes a while for me to hike down, but the bear is patient. Every so often, it stops and lifts a paw to encourage me forward. I get the feeling that if it knew me better, it would offer me a ride on its back.

I cannot believe this mountain. Who is training all these amazing bears? Maybe it's this mysterious brother, Everest. When I get back to Teddy, I'm going to grill him until he tells me.

I have no idea where Teddy's cabin is in relation to the original trail to the summit. But eventually the bear stops and snuffs at me, moving it's head from me to somewhere in front of it. I tiptoe past it and look down the hill through the pines. Below me is the parking lot with the black SUV rental car waiting for me.

"OMG," I squeal and turn to the polar bear. "Thank you." Teddy talked to the bear in his kitchen, so it feels natural to address this bear.

The bear bows its great, shaggy head. It raises a paw, and I wave back and watch as it lurches back into the forest, leaving not a leaf unturned in its wake.

Other than a fine layer of pollen coating the windshield, the SUV looks just as Bentley and I left it. I scramble down the hill towards it, pulling out my key fob from my bag. I still can't get over my amazing hike with an ursine tour guide. But the sooner I get my errands done, the sooner I can get back to Teddy.

I hit the unlock button, and the SUV chirps at me. There's my charger, in the front seat. Perfect. I can get my phone going and make some calls, then find my way into town for a change of underwear and directions back to Teddy's cabin.

I'm two feet away from the SUV's front door when someone bursts from the treeline above me, shouting.

"Lana!" It's Teddy. Startled, I watch with my mouth agape as he races down the hill and rushes up to me, moving faster than should be possible. At the last second, he bends forward and tackles me like a linebacker, hitching me onto his shoulder. My bag goes flying.

"Teddy, what the heck?" I'm ass up, face down, hanging over his shoulder, my braids raining down on his tight jean-clad butt. "I wasn't leaving for good. I just wanted to charge my phone!" I grab onto Teddy's t-shirt to steady myself as he whirls and heads away from the rental car. "Will you put me down?"

No answer. This is one determined mountain man.

"At least let me lock the door." I grunt and fight to raise my head to make sure the lights flash when I lock the door. We're a few yards away from the SUV. I lift the key fob and start mashing buttons, trying to relock the SUV. My finger slips and the horn blares. It'd be easier to do this if I was upright and not being carried by a crazy Viking. I try again and hit another button, the circular one that starts the car engine.

The world explodes in a blast of light and heat.

8

Teddy

The fireball rising from the remains of Lana's rental SUV sears my bare arms and the back of my neck.

I dive for the ground, whipping Lana around, so my body shields her from the explosion. I cover her with my bulk, my hands tucking her head into my shoulder. The move muffles her screams.

Fiery bits of metal rain down around us. One hits me in the back, and I arch and hiss, brushing it to the ground. My shifter healing can handle any flesh wounds. Lana's protection is my priority.

Someone must have rigged a car bomb to Lana's ignition. Either her brother or the assassin he hired. The explosion is over, leaving only the fire crackling along the ruined shell of the SUV and a sharp ringing in my ears.

I grabbed her just in time. There was a moment right before I came out of the trees when I registered that the car smelled strange. My instincts kicked in, and I let loose with shifter speed to save her. It doesn't matter that she saw my supernatural gifts in broad daylight. The only thing that matters is keeping her alive.

"OMG." Lana grips my t-shirt, shaking. She's hyperventilating.

"It's okay. I've got you." I lift off her and cup her face. "You're okay."

"What just happened?"

"A bomb."

The whine of a bullet is my only warning. I hunch over Lana, bracing to keep my weight off her as we hug the ground. A black object appears in the sky, hovering above an aspen tree. A drone. It's shooting at us.

Damn, her stepbrother's going all out. If the bomb didn't get her, the sniper's drone will.

A bullet ricochet skims my back. I bellow.

And my bear decides he's had enough. In one breath, I'm human. In the next, I'm a shaggy monster, with enough weight and girth to block Lana from the sunlight and burning air. My shout contorts in my throat, emerging as an inhuman roar.

My jeans and t-shirt are reduced to scraps of fabric littered around us in a radial pattern. Under me, Lana whimpers.

The drone is still armed and firing at will. Time to get the fuck out of here.

I lift Lana in a fireman's carry and hit top speed. I'm a werebear, and in bear form I'm faster than any creature alive. I have her most vulnerable areas—her head and torso—cradled in front of me, so I can protect her from bullets.

I leap into the forest and crash through the brush. The drone follows, joined by a second one. They're whizzing through the trees, shooting at us and trying to pin me down. Bullets buzz like angry hornets over our head. I tuck

Lana closer and put on a burst of shifter speed. Gotta get her out of here. Gotta keep her safe.

Nothing else matters.

~

LANA

The skin of my face feels like I've been lounging by the pool too long. The stench of burnt metal still lingers in my nostrils. I cough, hacking up smoke. I shudder, pressing close to the big shaggy creature that's carrying me.

My rental SUV just exploded. I'm pretty sure that's not covered by the travel insurance. But that's the least of my problems.

Someone is shooting at me and Teddy. I crane my neck, but I can't see the sniper. A bullet splinters the tree trunk next to me. I whimper and duck my head. Trees, rocks, bushes turn into a green-brown blend.

The furry monster grunts and tenses, hunching over me as it picks up speed. The wind rushes over me. We're moving so fast, my eyes are streaming. I whimper and duck my head, hanging onto the fur for dear life. I press my face into the soft shelter of its neck and breath. Teddy's scent hits my lungs.

Somehow this creature is Teddy. I saw it with my own eyes. One minute he was my surly Viking, racing out of the forest to rescue me. The next he turned into a creature. And not just any creature: a bear. The same brown bear I saw at the summit. It all comes rushing back.

At last, the bear slows. The world comes into focus. We're in a rocky crevice shadowed by a crop of pine. It's quiet, blissfully devoid of bullets and explosions. Safe.

Teddy puts me down and stands back on hind legs. And then his form shrinks back down until it's Teddy staring at me. A very naked Teddy, every muscle and colorful tattoo on full display.

"Teddy." I point a shaking finger at him. "You're a…"

"A bear," he confirms. His voice comes out a growl that's almost too low to be human. He clears his throat, his gaze intent on me. Normally grey, his eyes flash an eerie gold as they catch the light. "Are you okay? Were you hit?"

I splay my hands over my chest and look down taking inventory. "No, I'm not hit." I touch my forehead, half expecting to touch a bandage. Maybe I'm in the hospital, hallucinating all this. "What was that?"

"Someone was shooting at us. They were using drones."

"My car exploded."

"It's okay, babygirl. We got away. You're safe now."

I sag, suddenly exhausted. Teddy's brow wrinkles as I let myself slide down to the ground and lean against a rock. "Someone's trying to kill me. And you're…Teddy—you're a bear."

Teddy crouches in front of me, looking wary. "A werebear," he corrects.

Werebear. A human who turns into a bear. An actual bear. Shaggy fur, cute little ears.

"OMG," I whisper.

Teddy watches me closely. The sharp lines of his cheekbones, his blond brows and cropped hair, his wild beard—it's all so human. He's the same Teddy, a handsome, grouchy Viking.

But there's a creature lurking inside. The bear part of him. It's impossible, yet it's real. I feel the truth of it inside of me. I think of all the bears I've seen since I met him, and it all makes sense. His brothers—all of them—they must be werebears, too.

His gaze drops to the ground, and he seems…sad.

Biting my lip, I rise to my knees and scoot closer to him. I reach out and let my hand hover between us, wanting to touch his face but not daring to.

"Are you okay?" I whisper. "Does it hurt? When you…"

"Change," he supplies the word. "Or shift." He shakes his head. "No, it doesn't hurt."

I close the distance between us and cup his cheek with one hand. His skin is hot, feverish. It sears my palm but feels so good. He's alive. This is real.

"Teddy," I whisper. He presses into my palm, so I place my other hand on his opposite cheek and coax him forward. His scent hits me, pine and wild mint and a bit of smoke. Intoxicating like a shot of whiskey. "You saved me." I rest my forehead against his, needing more of his skin on mine. More of his scent and his heat. My lips brush his, and he groans.

"Lana," he says roughly and cups the back of my head, fisting a hand in my braids to pull me closer. And then we're in a clinch, me in his lap, trying to wrap myself around him while he draws my head back and kisses me so hard his beard burns my skin.

He twists and pushes me to my back, rearing over me in all his naked glory.

I reach for him, wriggling out of my hiking pants. "Teddy." I grab his shoulders, surging upward as I pull him close. My breasts are swollen, aching. I rub myself against him, trying to get relief. There are chafed patches all over my face, and I don't care. I want his beard to scratch every inch of my skin. I want him to pull my braids until my scalp aches. Until I know we're both alive.

TEDDY

Lana sighs into my mouth. I try to put some space in between us, and her nails nip at my bare ass. "Easy, babygirl. Just makin' sure you're comfortable."

"I need you in me now," she huffs. She doesn't seem overly shocked to discover I'm a bear. Nor does she have the scheming gleam Tiffany had. No, Lana just seems *turned on.*

Which makes resisting her impossible. I should be mourning the fact that she knows. That I will definitely have to mindwipe her now. Instead, all I can think about is sex.

I'm totally naked, and she's halfway there. She's lying on the ground with leaves caught on the crown of her head. I don't even have a blanket or a coat to spread under her.

She growls at me, loud enough to impress any werebear. I settle for stripping off the plaid shirt of mine she borrowed from this morning. The fabric already smells like her—honey and laurel mingling with my scent. The best scent in the world.

She's grabbing at me, greedy, and I catch both her small wrists with one hand, and cup the soft place between her legs with the other. The little murmur she makes me ache.

"I need to make you ready." I dip two fingers into her sweet pussy, hooking them around to find her g-spot. "Fuck, babygirl, you're dripping all over me." Her juices slick my palm. "I want you to come for me." I tweak her camisole down, baring her breasts. "Hands above your head," I order. As soon as I release her wrists, she stretches her arms up, pinning her own hands in place as if I tied her there. Her back arches, and her breasts rise in a breathtaking display.

"You're fucking perfect." I reward her, caressing one breast and rubbing my thumb over her pert nipple while I finger fuck her. "You're going to come, baby. Now. Come all over my hand. Let me feel you."

Her hips judder, twisting as she works herself on my fingers. I pinch her nipple, and dart my head forward to soothe the hurt with my tongue. I scrape my beard along the crevice between her breasts, and she convulses, coming all over my hand.

"Fuck, yes, baby. That's it." I keep stroking, teasing her higher.

"Good girl. Now. Hands and knees for me." I help her flip over, making sure she's kneeling on my plaid shirt. "It's my turn."

I stroke my cock into her silky heat, steadying her hips. She bows forward, bracing herself as I thrust harder and harder. "You're my good girl," I praise her as I rock her body forward with each thrust. "You take my cock so well."

"Yes, yes, yes," she whimpers. She rocks her knees wider and arches her back further.

I reach around her and palm the soft mound of her belly, sliding a hand down until I find the slick place between her legs. I rub her clit. "You're going to come again," I inform her. "You got that?"

"Yes, Teddy."

"Reach between your legs, rub yourself."

With a little gasp, she does as I command.

"Come again. Now."

I fondle her breast, teasing and pinching, listening closely to her breath catch. I keep sawing in and out of her in the same rhythm until her inner muscles ripple along my length. Her pussy clamps down on my cock so hard, I see stars.

Her wavering cry is the sweetest thing I've ever heard. I

catch hold of her braids with my free hand to draw her head back. "I'm going to fuck you hard now. And you're going to come. Over and over." I pull her up to her high knees. She's practically on my lap again, bounding on my cock as I slam into her, driving her forward. Her breasts bounce with every hard thrust.

I release her hair, and her head naturally lolls back on my shoulder, baring the sweet space between her shoulder and neck. I bow my head and nip at her skin, not quite drawing blood. *Yes,* my bear shouts. Fuck, I almost marked her again. It'd be so natural to let my fangs sink into her flesh and claim her forever. Leave my scent permanently embedded in her skin for all other shifters to recognize.

Instead, I snap my hips and stroke into her, hard and deep, over and over, until she's coming so much, I can't tell when one orgasm ends and the other begins.

At last, with a howl, I spend deep inside her. My cock spurts over and over, pumping her full. There's so much cum, I bet there's not an ounce of water left in my body when I'm done. And it's not enough. I want to mark her, right here, right now, and fuck her again until the imprint of my dick is on her womb.

"Lana." I tip her, so I can see her expression. She's limp in my arms, but there's a little smile on her face. I kiss her glowing cheeks and ease myself back, draping her over me so her soft skin is protected from the bare ground. The sun overhead is tucked behind a cloud, and the temp is cooling. We lie with arms and legs woven together, letting the flush of the moment fade, our heartbeats thumping as one.

I've run far and fast enough away that the drones can't find us. We're safe here for the moment. Eventually we'll need to move, but I just want to lie here with this perfect human in my arms.

A breeze kicks up, and Lana tucks herself into me.

"Cold?" I brush her braids back from her face, picking off pieces of brown leaves that cling to the glossy black and pink lengths.

"I'll be okay."

"We'll move soon."

"Teddy," she murmurs. "I hate to break the mood, but I have to know. When were you going to tell me that my stepbrother is trying to kill me?"

My chest deflates. "So you remember."

"I think I do," she says. "He had a knife and threatened me. I threw the urn at him, but I wasn't going to get away. And then…"

"A bear came out of the woods," I finish for her.

She wriggles around in the crook of my arm until she's facing me. "It was you, wasn't it?"

"I caught your scent in the woods, and I couldn't let him hurt you. I'll never let anyone hurt you."

"Why?"

Instead of answering, I dip my head and kiss her. The touch of her lips makes my dick stand to attention, so I stop before I roll her to her back and fuck her sore.

A little line creases the space between her eyebrows. I rub it with my thumb until it goes away.

"Why didn't you tell me what happened with Bentley?"

"I wanted to see if you remembered. And I didn't know how to explain without telling my part."

"That you can turn into a bear?"

I'm equally thrilled and dismayed to hear Lana say the words out loud. "It's a secret, babygirl. One this mountain has kept forever. Has to keep forever."

"I can't believe it." She stares into space. "Werebears are real. You're super fast," she adds absently.

"And strong. And I heal quickly."

"Like after the fight with your brother. Or the time you moved so fast across the room. Or that bullets hit you and haven't hurt you."

Man, I've fucked up so much. My bear kept acting out in front of her—the fucker. He wanted her to see him. He wanted her to know what I am.

Mate, my bear reminds me.

"What about the bear in your kitchen?" Lana asks. "And the polar bear, the one who was working with the beehives?"

There's a sinking feeling on my stomach followed by relief. Lana's smart. She's going to figure out everything, so I might as well tell her everything. I don't know what the future holds, but right now, I don't want any secrets between us.

"They're my brothers. The one in the kitchen was Axel. The polar bear is Everest."

"Everest," she breathes. "Hutch said his brother Everest would lead me to my car. A polar bear showed up. He acted very human."

"Yes. That's Everest."

Lana reaches up and smoothes my forehead with her thumb. She traces my features, studying them as if trying to find evidence of my bear.

"And what about the triplets? Hutch and Canyon and Bern? Matthias?"

"They're also shifters. Werebears. You haven't seen them in bear form yet." The trouble with telling Lana everything is that these are not just my secrets to tell. Everyone is affected when one of us reveals ourselves to a human. If that human decides to betray us, everyone is at risk.

"She wouldn't tell anyone," Hutch had argued. I have to agree. But nothing is certain.

"This is incredible," Lana is saying. "It's like I'm in a whole new world. One ruled by bears. I thought the bears around here were special. And they are." She giggles. "You're all werebears."

"Nothing special about us." She's so cute, I can't stop my smile.

"I disagree. OMG!" She squeaks and puts her hand over her mouth. "You have curtains with bears on them. I thought it was so cute you guys were sticking to a theme. Cute little bears everywhere."

"Hutch's idea of a joke. There's nothing little about me." I pull her close and press my dick into her backside, to remind her.

"No, there isn't," she murmurs. "But your bear is very cute."

I give her a squeeze and relax my head back to squint at the sky. My bear is preening.

She's still talking, sleepily musing, "Eight brothers, all werebears. Your mom must have gotten the best Christmas card photos."

Frost snakes down my spine. "No," I say, tense again. "No photos. This is a secret, and no one can know."

She rolls off me, scooting so she's facing me. "I understand," she vows, her eyes locking on mine.

I stare at her, searching her face.

"She wouldn't tell anyone," Hutch had said.

"You don't know that," I'd replied.

Lana looks solemn. "Teddy, I promise."

I should be happy. Lana is mine. But a flicker of doubt still burns. I've been here before, and it didn't end well.

I nod, reaching for her, but the moment is broken, and she's scrambling into her hiking pants. I sigh and rise. I'm going to have to run back naked.

I help Lana dress. She offers me back my own plaid

shirt, and I tie it around my waist. "What are we going to do about Bentley?"

"I have a team on it. They'll find him. In the meantime, it's not safe for you to be out here. C'mon." I hitch her into my arms. My cabin may or may not be compromised, but my brother's cabins are even better hidden. Which means, until we take out the assassin, we'll be bunking with them.

9

Lana

"We have to stop meeting like this." Matthias peers at my scalp. I'm on a couch in a new, bigger cabin that belongs to the Terrible Threes and the mysterious brother Axel. "This is the cabin we were raised in," Teddy told me. He seemed distracted, so I held off asking for a tour. From my perch on the couch, the cabin looks similar to Teddy's, made of hewn pine and filled with worn, well-loved furniture. The main difference is the bigger fireplace and the extra rooms radiating off the main space.

Teddy's outside now, on the phone. I overheard him talking to someone named Deke and asking for "clean up" and decided I didn't need to hear anymore. Then Matthias came in carrying his black bag and checked me out.

"I'm okay." I smile up at Matthias. "Just a little shaky."

"That's to be expected." He slots his instruments back into his black bag and peels off his gloves. "Your head looks fine. No new injuries. I'd prescribe rest and avoiding stress for the next few days, but something tells me you might find that difficult."

"It's okay. I've never had anyone trying to kill me, but I've never had a werebear protecting me before, either."

"It's a good sign you have all your memories back. We were wondering what you would remember." Matthias gives me a meaningful look.

"I'm not going to tell anyone. I promise."

"That's good, Lana. It's not only Teddy's secret. Our entire family's safety depends on your silence."

"I understand. I'd never say anything. I know how to keep a secret." I fold my hands like a good little girl repeating what the adults want to hear. Teddy seems so much more tense since getting back to the cabin, and something tells me it's not just because he's trying to track down the assassin. Sharing a secret of a lifetime is a big deal.

"Good." Matthias adjusts his glasses, and the angle makes the lenses opaque, hiding his eyes. "Because if you do, there will be consequences."

I gulp.

"I don't want to scare you," Matthias gentles his tone, "but we have to take our privacy seriously."

"Of course. I take it seriously too. I promise." I twist my fingers together. I thought Teddy and his other brothers were badass, and Matthias was the smart, scholarly one, but I'm squirming under his stern gaze. He could crack a terrorist in two minutes, no show of force necessary. "Are there any other humans who know?"

"A small handful. Most of them are mates of shifters."

"Mates?"

"Shifters have mates."

"Like a soulmate?"

"Similar. The concept of a soulmate in the human world is a cute idea for romantics, but for us shifters, it's the most important thing in the world. A shifter's mate is the one person in the world meant for him or her. When a shifter finds a mate, the animal self accepts the person immediately. They're meant to be together. For life. It's Fate."

"Fate," I repeat in a whisper.

Hadn't Teddy muttered something about fate after the first time we had sex?

I squeeze my arms around myself to contain the giddiness welling up in me. Am I Teddy's mate? The only one in the world meant for him? It would be the most wonderful thing that's happened to me. I want it to be true.

I want to ask a million questions, but they can wait for Teddy.

"All done?" Teddy's in the doorway, holding the phone he borrowed from Matthias.

"Patient's checked out. All good."

I give Teddy a little wave and beckon for him to come to my side. The line of his shoulders is rigid, but he prowls to me right away and drops to the couch to tuck me into his side. Immediately we both relax.

Mate. The word bounces around my skull, filling me with warmth and drunken butterflies. I sensed a connection with Teddy from the beginning. Does the mate thing go both ways?

"I have good news, and I have bad news," Canyon says. "The good news is we found the drones and destroyed them."

Teddy groans. "Is at least one of them in one piece?"

"No," Hutch says. "Canyon invented a new game called 'Smash the drone with a branch into a rock'."

"It's like baseball, but the ball is shooting at you," Canyon adds.

"Sorry." Hutch hands Teddy a cloth sack full of clinking contents. "We got a little carried away."

Teddy reaches into the sack and pulls out a shiny black shard that's smaller than a phone. The sad remains of the drone. "Damn it. We could've used this to track the assassin." Teddy scrubs a hand over his close-cropped head. "I'll give this to the Black Wolf pack and see what they can do." Teddy tosses the piece back into the bag. "Was that the bad news?"

"Uh, no," Canyon says, "there's more."

"Where's Bern?"

"He's with Everest. Did you call your Black Wolf pack crew about cleanup? Because I have some other coordinates for them. Longitude and latitude."

"What did you do?" Teddy growls.

"It was Everest," Hutch says. "He meant well. He's the one who pointed us towards the drones. He heard the explosion and saw them hunting you. We took them out."

"Yeah," Canyon interrupts. "It was awesome. They were whizzing around, and we were all like—" He karate chops the air, making *"pew pew"* shooting noises.

"Canyon." Hutch makes slashing motion across his throat.

Canyon stops his dramatic re-telling of events, dropping his hands when he notices Teddy's glare. "Sorry."

"Anyway," Hutch continues. "Everest told us about the explosion. He was watching from the woods. In fact, he's the one who said that the SUV smelled a little funny when he brought Lana to it in the first place."

"Then why did he bring her and leave her there?" Teddy bursts out.

I put a hand on his back, rubbing it, and he falls silent, closing his eyes and squeezing the bridge of his nose. "Nevermind."

"Well," says Hutch, "Everest went ahead and followed

the scent trail. So while the assassin was sending his drones after you, Everest was hunting him."

"Please tell me you got him."

"Sort of." Hutch shoots a guilty glance in my direction.

Teddy sees it and leans back, putting his arm around me. "You can speak freely in front of Lana. She knows everything now."

"Oh yeah?" Canyon and Hutch break into identical grins. "Welcome to the family."

"Thanks." I smile back. Beside me Teddy is tense, but of course he is, after all we've been through. I take his hand and squeeze it, and the rigid line of his shoulder eases.

"Anyway, Everest chased him. And the assassin was already freaked out or something—"

"If he had a visual through the drone, he saw me shift," Teddy explains.

There's a pause as the brothers digest this. "Then it's kind of good what happened," Hutch says. "Everest went after the assassin and accidentally chased him over a cliff."

Teddy hangs his head, covering his face with his hand.

"Did he survive?" Matthias asks.

"No, he is very much dead," Hutch says.

I squeak and put a hand over my mouth. All the brothers look at me. "Well," I say, when I can find my voice. "It couldn't have happened to a nicer person."

"Ha, yeah." Hutch bobs his head and looks at Teddy. "That's why I need to give you the coordinates where he is. Everest and Bern are waiting with the body."

"Right." Teddy hands over his phone to Canyon. "Hit redial and ask for more cleanup."

"SA-weet!" Canyon grabs the phone and disappears outside.

"Is there any other equipment that you found?" Teddy asks Hutch.

"No, but we can go check it out."

"Anything we find, we can give to the Black Wolf pack in case it helps them trace the assassins."

I blow out a breath. This is the most bizarre conversation I've ever had, and that includes one with a film producer and my brand manager who wanted to shoot a GoddessWear commercial with trained peacocks, a space shuttle launch and models lounging in a pool filled with red Jello. As weird marketing a fashion brand can be, this day filled with assassins and finding out the existence of bear shifters outstrips them all.

"Do you think the assassin was working with a team?" Matthias wonders.

"Maybe," Teddy says. "But now, my gut says the drones were probably his team."

"Does that mean it's over?" I ask.

Silence. Teddy's arm tightens around me. "It could be. My friends–the Black Wolf pack–are experts. They're trying to track Bentley."

Bentley. I twist my fingers together. "You know for sure he's behind this?"

"Lana." Teddy takes hold of my chin and turns me to look at him. "Other than the assassin, your stepbrother is the only person who's tried to kill you in the past forty-eight hours. I'd say this is him escalating."

Damn. It's one thing to be part of a dysfunctional family. It's another thing to come to terms with the fact your stepbrother is trying to kill you for your inheritance.

I swallow.

Teddy's thumb strokes along my cheek. "I'm going to protect you, babygirl."

"I know you will," I whisper back.

He presses his forehead to mine. His scent hits me, and all the stress in my body melts to nothing.

"You smell so good." I dart my head to his neck to give him a good sniff. "When this is all over, I'm going to bottle this scent and make it into a line of candles."

"Lana."

"Don't worry." I hug him closer. "They will be very manly candles. And I'd never reveal my trade secret inspiration."

I can't see his face, but I can feel his cheek curve into a smile.

"All done." Canyon bursts back into the cabin, holding Teddy's phone aloft. "Deke says they'll take care of it."

"Deke is such a bad ass," Hutch says, and Canyon agrees.

"Who's Deke?" I ask.

"Friend of mine, from my unit," Teddy answers.

"In the Army?"

"Yeah. He's a wolf shifter," Canyon bursts out. "Part of the Black Wolf pack. They live up in Taos."

"There are wolf shifters?" I turn wide eyes to Teddy. "Like…werewolves?"

"They turn into wolves instead of bears, so yeah." Teddy strokes the side of my thigh.

"Wow." I wriggle in my seat. Heat curls through me with every pass of Teddy's teasing fingers. He's looking at me like he wants to carry me away from his brothers, off to a secluded location. I want that too, but right now, my curiosity gets the best of me. "This is all so incredible. There's a whole world out there I never knew about. How have you been able to keep it a secret?"

Teddy's fingers still.

"We're pretty good at keeping hidden," Matthias says.

"And if a human finds out what they're not supposed to know, there are ways to make sure they forget."

Well, that doesn't sound ominous at all.

I shrink into Teddy and drop that line of questioning.

"The important thing is, the assassin is dealt with," Teddy says. "And we survived."

Hutch clears his throat. "Actually, we haven't finished telling you all the good news and bad news. That was actually all good news. We haven't gotten to the bad news yet."

Teddy's rubbing his forehead again. "What now?"

"The real bad news is that Daisy came to your cabin shortly after you left. She's calling an emergency town meeting. Darius is going to be there."

"Darius?" I repeat. Teddy's chest rumbles with a growl.

"Yeah. Daisy says Darius is presenting his idea to save the town. We're all supposed to vote on it."

"When?" Teddy barks.

"Tonight."

"I'll talk to her," Matthias says. "See if she can put it off."

Hutch scratches his head. "I don't know, big bro. Daisy's pretty determined. She says it's time to put up or shut up. And Darius flew in."

"All right," Teddy rumbles. "First things first. We coordinate with the Black Wolf pack. Make sure we clean up our mess."

"What about the town meeting?" Canyon asks. "Do you want Darius to win?"

"Fine," Teddy grouses. "If everything goes well in the next few hours, we'll all show up to vote. But I think we can all agree, keeping Lana safe is a priority."

His brothers chorus assent, and all the warm fuzzies filling me threaten to make me burst into tears.

10

Lana

After a few precious minutes cuddling with Teddy on the couch, he gets a text from the Black Wolf pack.

"They need me for a debrief." He pockets his phone with a sigh. "I need to go. You need to stay here, where it's safe."

"Okay," I say. "I'll be okay."

"I'll be back as soon as I can, babygirl." Teddy kisses me, once on the lips, once on the forehead.

"I'll just take a little nap." I cover my mouth to hide a yawn. "I'm tired." And overwhelmed. Not even because of all the bombshells exploding everything I thought I knew about the world or the attempt on my life but because of the way Teddy and his brother's have welcomed me. After years of my immediate family freezing me out, I feel like I've come in from the cold. Like I've been taken in.

"You can nap right here. Hutch and Canyon will be around. They'll get you what you need." Teddy kisses me again and turns to point a finger at two of the Terrible Threes. "I'm trusting you to keep Lana safe."

Hutch and Canyon draw themselves up to attention. "Sir, yes, sir!" Canyon throws a salute. "We'll guard her with our lives."

"An army could show up to get her, and we'd fight them all off."

"Victory or die!"

"Okay. Good," Teddy says. "I'm counting on you." He ducks out of the cabin, and I dash the tears from my eyes before Hutch and Canyon see.

I end up falling asleep right on the couch. When I wake, I'm covered in a blanket. Hutch is moving around the kitchen, but no one else is around.

Hutch hears me stirring and comes over with a glass of water. I take it with a murmured, "Thank you," and tip the glass to hide my smile. These Bad Bear brothers are such gentlemen.

Hutch hovers at my side. "Did you sleep well?"

"I did. Did I miss anything?"

"Nope. Teddy's not back yet, but he should be soon. Canyon and I are going to make dinner. Grilled salmon and salad with goat cheese and blueberries."

"That sounds good."

"It's Teddy's favorite. After dinner, we're all going to the town meeting. Matthias couldn't convince Daisy to move it, so Teddy ordered all hands on deck. All of us will be there to stop Darius. Every vote counts."

I sit up and push my braids back. "And this meeting is about saving the mountain?"

"Yep." Canyon pokes his head out of the hall.

"So, in all the excitement, I haven't had a chance to ask. Why is it so important to stop Darius? You say you need to save the mountain, but why? Who's threatening it?"

"It's a long story." Canyon pads over and plops into a

worn armchair facing the couch. "It all came down to the town council needing money to do some things. They wanted to build some new roads. Fix the water tower, upgrade the sewer system, stuff like that. They took out some loans."

"Issued a bond," Hutch corrects. "That's how they put it."

"Whatever." Canyon waves a hand. "Unfortunately the bond got bought by some cutthroat hedge fund. And now they want all their money back."

"Plus an insane amount of interest," Hutch says. "Daisy said she'd rather owe the cartel than a hedge fund."

"Yikes. I know what she means," I say. GoddessWear gets its fair share of offers from interested investors, including hedge funds. Cutthroat is a polite way to describe them. "So how much do you have to pay back?"

"Like ten million," Hutch tells me. "For a small town, it's a huge amount."

"But it's okay," Canyon kicks back and puts his boots on the coffee table. "We can make the money back. I have tons of ideas."

Hutch snorts. "We've tried everything. We started keeping chickens, so we could sell the eggs. But we eat most of them."

Canyon pats his bare stomach. "I'm a growing bear."

"Sure you are." Hutch rolls his eyes.

Canyon sits up and snaps his fingers. "What about the beehives? We could sell the honey."

"Oh, that'd be cute," I pipe up. "I can see the logos now: Bad Bear Bee Farm."

"No," Bern says. "Everest doesn't want to let us take any honey. He's too attached to the bees. Besides, how are we going to make ten million selling goods at a farmer's market? We need to brainstorm another way." He props his chin in his hands, looking glum. "Teddy has a helicopter business, but he's not looking to expand yet."

"And after today's little joyride, he's probably not letting me near his bird anytime soon." Canyon looks equally glum.

"Too bad," I say. "I could sew you some matching jumpsuits."

"Matching jumpsuits?" Hutch says. "Aww, man. We gotta convince Teddy."

"Good luck with that," Canyon says. "The point is we need to find a way to get our hands on the money fast."

"Got it. And how does Darius come in?"

"He has plans to pay back the debt, but they all involve selling tracts of land to build condos."

I ponder this. "That isn't necessarily a bad thing. There's a housing shortage, and if they were built sustainably—"

Canyon makes a face. "Teddy says all Darius cares about is making money. I wouldn't bet on him doing anything that cuts into his bottom line."

"Gotcha."

"Darius is going to present his plans to pay back the debt tonight," Canyon continues. "And we'll all vote on it. The thing is, we have to come up with an alternative, otherwise people might vote for what Darius wants. Also, Teddy thinks that Darius engineered all of this, so he could get the town to agree to his condo idea. And guess who owns the real estate company who would build the condos?"

"Darius?"

"Darius."

"Got it." Now it all makes sense. Teddy's hatred of his twin, the way he blamed Darius for the mountain's problems. "Teddy thinks Darius engineered all of this to get the town in a position to agree to build the condos?"

"Something like that. I gotta hand it to Darius—his plan is better than what the hedge fund wants to do," Hutch says. "If we default, they'll probably take over, implement austerity measures, and sell off parts of the mountain for logging."

I grimace. "That's no good."

"No. It'll destroy our habitat."

Both Hutch and Canyon look so down, I clap my hands, making them jump. "Guys! We can turn this around. We can raise the money."

"But ten million dollars?"

"We can do it. We can figure something out. I can think of a few ideas, but first and most importantly, I need your help with something."

The two triplets look alert.

"Even if I can think up a way to raise money for the mountain and convince Teddy to take me, what am I going to wear?"

"I can help with that." Hutch jumps up. "Wait here." He returns lugging a vintage black sewing machine with the Singer logo emblazoned on the side.

"OMG," I scoot to the edge of the couch. "Does it work?"

"Oh yeah. It's Ma's. She taught us how to use it." He sets the heavy machine on the coffee table in front of me. "Now we just need fabric."

I smile. "I have some ideas."

~

Teddy

"And that's a wrap." Lance, one of the Black Wolf

pack's shifters and former member of my unit in the Army, grabs the back door to the van we've been working out of and slams it shut. "No more body. And for my next trick, I'll make the bombed out car disappear."

"Thank you." My bear is itching to get back to Lana's side.

Lance sees me fidgeting, and his face splits into a grin. "Oh, and welcome to the club."

"Club?"

"The mated shifter club. Lana's your mate, right?"

I hesitate. I haven't marked her. But of course, the urge is there. I can't pretend any more that it's not true. She's definitely my mate.

"Yeah." It feels good to admit it. But damn, if it fills me with fear.

"Yeah," Lance repeats, nodding at the look at my face. "Trust me, I know exactly what you're feeling right now. Happy and crazy all at once."

I pinch the bridge of my nose. "It's just...she's so fragile."

"You'd be protective of her even if she wasn't human. She's got an assassin targeting her. And even if she didn't, you'd still want to lock her in a bunker and hide her from the world."

"Sounds about right. Speaking of which, what intel do you have on Lana's stepbrother?"

Lance's jovial mood drops away. "We're still tracking Bentley Dupree. He's smart. He's gone into hiding. I bet he does that until he knows Lana is dead."

"We can make him believe that." Rafe approaches with Deke behind him. Deke's wearing dark aviator shades and coiling up some rope. I have no idea what he needed rope for, and I don't want to know.

Rafe nodes to me. "Our next step is to make Dupree think Lana's dead."

"How?"

"We have Channing and a few insiders working on cracking the assassin's communication lines. We can send a message to Dupree from the assassin, requesting payment and saying the mission is complete. That should bring him out of hiding. Then we'll get him."

"All right. It's a plan."

"It'll be all right, brother." Lance slaps me on the back and leans in for a half-hug. I bump shoulders with him and return the back slap and do the same with Rafe.

"Thank you, brother." I flick my fingers in salute to Deke, who nods.

"And we'll have you and Lana up to visit soon," Rafe adds. "Adele and the ladies will want to meet her. They can talk to her, help her acclimate to shifter matehood faster."

"That sounds good. She'll probably like that."

"She'll need that," Lance says. "Our mates are badass, but no question, taking a human mate has some complications."

"That's a fucking understatement," Deke mutters.

"Humans complicate everything." Lance shrugs. "But it's worth it. You got this." With a final slap on my back, Rafe and the rest climb into their vehicles and head out.

I raise a hand to send them off. Lance, Deke and Rafe all took human mates, and it worked out for them. They trust. But they don't know that I've been down this road before.

Tiffany was human. And she betrayed me.

Lana isn't Tiffany. I never felt like this with Tiffany.

My bear is content in the knowledge that Lana is our mate. I can be, too.

Lana

An hour later, I have a makeshift skirt pieced together from a donated pair of jeans. Hutch hovers over my shoulder while I pin things in place and give him pointers.

"Can I ask a personal question?" I ask Hutch around the needles in my mouth, and wait for his nod and shrug. "Where is your mom?"

"Ma? She's good. She has her own place now, for privacy. She's hibernating."

"Hibernating?"

"A few days after we turned eighteen, she said she loved us, but she'd raised seven boys, eight if you count Everest, and she needed a break. She's been sleeping on and off since then."

"Oh, wow." That sounds nice, actually. I wouldn't mind being able to hibernate every once in a while. "Wait, why wouldn't you count Everest as a boy she raised?"

"She didn't really adopt him. He wandered out of the woods one day and sat down to eat at our picnic table. Everest is like that. He comes around when he wants, and when he stays away no one can find him. But he's still part of the family."

"Family," I murmur. I love their family. Mine was nothing like this.

"Hey, guys, you almost done?" Canyon calls from the kitchen. "Teddy texted that he's on his way. I've got the grill prepped and need some help. We gotta eat now if we're going to make it to the town meeting."

"I'll be ready." I whip my new jean skirt away from the sewing machine and hold it up. "Just give me a sec to change."

This time, instead of watching the seamless choreography of prepping for dinner, I'm a part of it. Me and the two Bad Bear brothers work in sync to get the salad stock chopped and the salmon on the grill. Hutch and I stream back and forth from the kitchen to the picnic tables, setting out plates, utensils and napkins.

Matthias and Bern show up first. The goth triplet takes a heavy stack of plates out of my arms and ferries them to the right spots.

"You should be resting." Matthias peers at me.

"I napped," I say. "I'm feeling fine, I promise."

"Hey, Lana, sit over here," Canyon waves. "You'll be next to Teddy and me."

I beam at him and take my spot. It's like having four new brothers. A whole new family.

Be careful, a little voice inside me cautions. *It might not last.* But I wave that little voice away. I need to think positive.

Matthias checks his phone and pockets it. "Teddy's coming. He says to start dinner without him."

"He better get here quick," Canyon warns. "Otherwise, there's no time for him to eat before the town meeting."

"Plus, Everest will scarf all his salmon." Bern digs the tongs into the salad and serves me.

"Everest is coming?" I perk up. "I've been wanting to meet him. Outside of bear form, I mean."

"He's great," Hutch sets a bread basket near me. "Really quiet. Kind of shy. He'll come to the meeting with us. Between him and Teddy, you'll be perfectly safe, Lana."

"What about us?" Canyon protests.

"And us. We'll guard you."

Matthias sets down his fork. "You're coming to the meeting?"

"I want to," I say. "If Teddy thinks it's safe."

Canyon nudges me. "Here's Everest."

A shadow falls over the table. I shield my eyes to look into the setting sun, and the giant blocking it.

Everest is a mountain of a man with tan skin and a full beard that rivals Teddy's. He gives me a solemn nod and raises a hand, and I immediately see the resemblance to the huge polar bear who waved shyly at me from behind the beehives.

The angry buzz of an engine sends a flock of birds fluttering from the trees. A black dirt bike zooms up to us and brakes hard. A spray of dirt showers against the cabin's side. The rider pulls off his helmet and spends a second shaping his black hair into a mohawk before loping over to the picnic tables.

"And this is Axel," Matthias introduces me to the last of the Bad Bear brothers. "I think you've also met him in bear form."

"He was the black bear in the kitchen," Hutch murmurs.

"Oh," I say and straighten. "Hello. I'm Lana."

Axel tugs off his leather jacket, revealing two full sleeves of tattoos. He's tall as the teens but more filled out. With his high forehead and full lips, he looks like a slouchy James Dean, if the rebel without a cause was played by Daniel Henney. "Hey." He jerks up his chin in greeting and starts to take the spot next to me.

"No, dude. That's Teddy's seat," Hutch says. Canyon throws his arms out to block Axel from sitting.

"Lana's Teddy's girl," Bern explains.

"Oh yeah?" Axel regards me sleepily and prowls to the other end of the table to take a seat near Everest. "Another human?"

Did he say...*another* human?

Silence falls on the table. My mouthful of salmon turns dry. Is dating a human taboo?

"What do you mean *another*?" I ask, but no one answers.

"The best human," Hutch defends.

"Don't be rude," Matthias murmurs to Axel, who shrugs. "Sorry."

"It's okay. I am human." I give a little shrug.

"It's cool. You can't help it," Bern says, which doesn't make me feel better.

"She has ideas about how to save the mountain," Hutch pipes up.

"Oh?" Matthias looks over the top of his glasses at me.

I swallow my bite of salmon quickly. "Um, I have a few, but I'm still working on them."

"It'll be a surprise," Canyon saves me. "Me and Hutch are going to help present it."

"That's good," Matthias encourages.

I look down at my plate. I hope so. I don't want to let anybody down.

Other than the clattering of dishes and a few murmurs of *pass the salt*, the next few minutes are quiet as the Bad Bear brothers fall into their food. Salmon and salad and whole loaves of bread disappear as fast as Hutch and Canyon can replenish them. I pick at my food. Axel's comment reminds me how little I know about shifter culture. Being a shifter is a closely guarded secret. Teddy and Matthias made that clear. It makes sense that shifter-human relationships are rare. When Matthias told me about some shifters having human mates, it gave me hope, but I might have gotten excited too soon.

What if I'm not Teddy's mate? What if there's a shifter out there for him?

And if I am Teddy's mate, can we make it work? Or

will me being human be a rift that grows and keeps us apart?

I really, really want Teddy here, now. When I'm with him, I don't think. I don't stress. I just feel. I can be myself, and I am enough.

Teddy's scent hits me before I hear his voice. "There's my girl."

Teddy. I turn in relief and close my eyes as he kisses my forehead.

"Are these bad bears treating you right?"

"Yes." I push up to give him a proper kiss.

"You're late." Hutch skewers a salmon steak, slaps two pieces of bread around it, and hands it to Teddy. "Eat up. We've got to go if we're going to get to the town meeting in time."

Teddy tears into his salmon sandwich. "You look nice," he tells me between bites.

"Thank you," I preen. I lean back to show him my new jean skirt and the t-shirt of Teddy's that I altered, so the collar dips off one shoulder.

"She wanted a new outfit to go to the meeting," Hutch says.

Teddy chokes. "Baby, no," he says. "It's not safe."

"Why not?" Canyon demands. "The assassin is lying dead at the bottom of a ravine. If he comes back to life as a zombie, we'll just take him out again." He punches the air. Bern dodges his brother's fist to grab the last of the bread.

At the far end of the table, Everest raises his hands and cracks the knuckles of his huge fist. The sound is like distant gunshots.

"See?" Canyon points to the largest of the Bad Bear brothers. "Everest would love another round with an assassin. He's ready."

"What did the Black Wolf Pack say about the situation?" Matthias asks.

"They're cracking the assassin's comm codes, so they can get a message to Lana's stepbrother," Teddy says. "The one who called the hit. See if they can flush him out."

"So it's fine," Canyon argues. "It's just a little ole town meeting. There'll be barely anyone there. We'll be with her. She'll be perfectly safe."

"Now is the safest time for her to go," Hutch adds. "Her brother still hasn't realized that she's alive."

I realize I'm toying with the neck of my newly altered shirt and drop my hand. "What do you think Bentley'll do when he finds out I'm not dead?"

"Doesn't matter. We'll take care of it," he says.

"Which reminds me about one of my ideas to raise money for the mountain. Lana, I didn't tell you about this earlier because I figured it would be classified, but now you're part of the family." Canyon waits until he has everyone's attention, and announces, "Picture this: werebear assassins."

"Hell, yeah." Bern thumps the table.

"Rock on," Axel mumbles around a mouthful of food. Everest cracks his knuckles again.

"No," Teddy and Matthias say in unison. "Absolutely not,"

"Aw, come on," the three triplets groan. "It'll be so cool. We can work on our fight skills."

"Bern can get better at flying the helicopter," Hutch says. Bern nods his head so hard, his hair flops back into his face.

"Think about it," Canyon urges.

"I don't have to think about it," Teddy said. "If I let you guys do wet work, Ma would kill me."

Canyon drops back in his seat. "Ma's hibernating. She doesn't have to know."

I bite my lip to keep from smiling.

"Let's clean up." Teddy swirls his finger over the remains of dinner. His own sandwich has disappeared. "We gotta get to the meeting."

"So wait." Canyon springs out his chair again. "We're just going to leave Lana behind?"

Teddy hesitates. "I'll stay with her."

"When I talked to Daisy it seemed like the town was pretty split over this decision to go with Darius's plan," Matthias says. "About half and half. It'll probably come down to a few votes to decide which way we go."

"Every vote counts," Hutch says. "We all gotta go. It's our last chance to save the mountain."

I push out my lower lip in a pout. "Please?"

Teddy rubs his forehead.

I swallow. "Nevermind. It's okay." I grab an empty bread basket and hustle to the cabin.

"Lana…Lana, wait." He catches up right before I scramble inside, blocking the door. The rest of his brothers stream past us, cleaning up dinner. I keep my head down to hide my tears.

"Here." Teddy leads me off to the side of the cabin, where we can have some privacy. "I need to keep you safe."

"I'd be safe. I'd be with all of you. Will I really be safer alone in the cabin? And don't say you'll leave someone to watch me. You all need to be at the meeting."

Teddy growls. "This fucking meeting—"

"Is important. It's important to you. I know I'm a burden—"

"Fuck, Lana, you're not a burden. I didn't mean to imply that."

"I know. I know it's not ideal. I just wanted to h-help." My voice hitches.

"Come here." He takes the bread basket I'm still holding, tosses it away and wraps me in his arms.

I press into him, grateful for his hug. "You guys have helped me so much, and now I can support you. This is important to you, and I want to be a part of it. It's nice to be a part of something."

Teddy grips me tight, muttering a curse.

"You guys are a family. It's awesome. Just what a family should be. At least, what I think a family should be. Mine was never like that, no matter how much I wanted it."

"Baby. I'm sorry."

"It's okay."

"No, it's not." He releases me to cup my face. "You're little miss sunshine, and you haven't been treated the way you should be. I'm sorry your parents died, and your brother's competing for murderous asshole of the century."

"Thank you."

"You deserve the family of your dreams."

"I think I found it," I whisper against his lips, and he tilts his head to kiss me. His big hands slide around to cup my ass. I find myself suspended off the ground, straddling Teddy's thigh. I wrap my legs around his hips and let him plunder my mouth.

My nipples get hot and tingly where they press up against his chest.

"You sure about that?" he asks when we come up for air. He lets me down, and I push my braids back. "You're okay with putting up with my brothers, if it means you can be with me?"

"I like your brothers."

"That makes one of us." Teddy sees my face and adds,

"I'm kidding. I like my brothers. Especially Everest. He doesn't talk my ear off. I just don't know, out of all the places on the mountain, why he'd built his beehives over by mine."

"I expect it's the same reason Axel keeps his sausage in your fridge, and the Terrible Threes keep bugging you about bagpipe practice. They like you. They're your family. They want to be close to you. That's what families do." Crap, I'm going to cry again. All at once, I feel moved by the thought of being one of them and sad because no matter how hard I tried, Bentley and even my parents, never wanted anything to do with me. I blink rapidly.

"Babygirl." Teddy wraps me in his arms again. "I'm sorry. I'll stop complaining about them. I love my brothers... they just drive me nuts."

"From what I hear, that's also what families do." I squeeze him tighter. "Viking hugs make it all better." My breasts ache, wanting to brush against his hard chest. Instead, I pull away and straighten my shirt, twitching the boat neck into place. "But let's get to this meeting."

Teddy groans. "I want to carry you off to a secluded cabin, keep you there for a week."

"That sounds good."

"Tonight, I'm kicking the triplets out of their cabin, and it's going to be you and me, alone."

"Okay," I whisper. "As long as the triplets are fine with it."

"They don't have a choice."

"That's okay," a muffled voice reaches us. I look around, but can't find the source. Above our heads, a window scrapes and Hutch's head pops out. "We can sleep in the woods for a few nights."

I gasp and grip Teddy, who clutches me close and thunders at his brother, "This is a private conversation!"

"We're shifters, remember?" Canyon's muffled voice comes from behind Hutch. "We can hear everything you're saying."

"Really?" I mouth to Teddy.

He nods, looking tired. "See why I want to get you alone?"

There's an argument happening above our heads. Hutch disappears and Bern sticks his head out. "Hey, Lana, I've got an idea. Here." He tosses down a black hoodie. "She can wear this. No pink." He motions to me. "Tuck in your hair." When I do, he nods approvingly. "Stealth mode."

"See." Canyon squeezes his face next to Bern. "Now she's in disguise. It'll be totally safe."

"No one's filming the presentation," Hutch adds. "It won't be broadcasted. And Daisy makes everyone turn off their phones at the beginning of a meeting."

Teddy crosses his burly arms across his chest. "I still don't like it."

"Please, Teddy." I step in front of him and lean in, looking up through my eyelashes. "The second you think there's danger, you can get me out. I'll follow your lead."

"You'll stay close to me," he says.

"Yes." Above me, in the window, the triplets have found a way to squeeze all three of their heads through the frame. We all wait, holding our breath.

Teddy grunts, "Fine."

"Yay!" I clap my hands. "You guys ready to do this?"

"Hell yeah," chorus the triplets.

"Does a bear shit in the woods?" Canyon adds.

I cock my head and raise my brows at him.

"We do," Hutch confirms. Beside him, Bern is nodding. "We definitely do."

11

Teddy

I grip Lana's hand and lead her back to the picnic tables. Everyone's done their part, and traces of dinner have been cleared away.

Lana whistles. "Your Ma trained you boys well."

"Yep." I give a two fingered salute to Matthias and Everest, who melt into the woods. Lana starts to follow, but I stop her short.

"This way, babygirl."

She wrinkles her nose, trotting next to me. "We're not going to hike down?"

"Nope." I head over to the shed, passing Axel starting his dirtbike. He nods to us, and zooms off, and I find the tracks I'm looking for, and follow them behind the cabin where a tarp covered ATV waits. I pull off the covering. "We'll ride in this. It's in pretty good shape."

"Is it?" Lana looks skeptical. The ATV is a Frankenstein machine with huge, mud spattered wheels, a roll cage, and a bench seat and other parts cannibalized from a golf cart.

I boost her into the seat, kissing her on the lips. "Can you hang on, babygirl?"

"Of course."

I can't hold her hand and steer, but the seat is small enough and the back road is bumpy enough, Lana slides in close, hanging on to me. My bear approves. He wants to keep his paws on her at all times. He also wants me to turn this ATV around and find a safe cave for us to hide in for the next decade. It doesn't help that I think this is a good idea.

Compromise.

"You okay?" Lana has her hand on my knee. My whole body is rigid.

I nod, unable to find my voice to answer her. As we roll down the road, I scan the route for threats. Every noise and fluttering leaf makes me sweat.

Lana must sense my tension because she asks, "Are you worried about Darius?"

"A little."

She rubs my knee. "It'll be okay. The meeting will go fine."

I catch her hand and press a kiss to the palm. "It will be. Thank you, babygirl. But after this outing, we lie low," I say firmly.

"Agreed. But…for how long? As much as I want to hole up somewhere with you for a month, eventually I will have to let my team know where I am and my plans for coming back from vacation."

Right. Lana isn't a Viking hermit, like me. She's famous and runs a company.

"We'll figure it out." It'll be another compromise my bear won't like. *Humans make things complicated, but that doesn't mean it can't work.*

Lana goes quiet. "Do you think your friends will be able to stop Bentley?"

I stop the ATV, turn and cup her face. I kiss her like I want to mark her mouth. "They won't rest until they do. I'm not going to let anything happen to you. I promise you. I'm going to protect you from him, from everyone. You're not alone."

∼

LANA

I'm two seconds away from losing my nerve and asking Teddy to take me back, make love to me until we forget about the town, his brother and mine. But that's not fair. Teddy's helped me so much. It's my turn to help him.

"Thank you." I steady myself. "Let's get this show on the road."

Teddy's about to put the ATV in gear when to our right, in the trees, someone whoops and hollers. I cringe against Teddy, but it's only the triplets. They come bursting out of the forest and run past us, slapping the golf cart.

"Dumbasses," Teddy mutters, but there's a smile on his voice.

"I think they're sweet."

Teddy grunts and swivels his head. "Get off, Canyon!" he shouts.

The shirtless teen is gripping the back of the ATV. He cackles and swings from the roll bar and then scampers off. The sun is setting, and in the low light, two kilted forms and one in full black sprint and weave across the road in front of us all the way into the town of Bad Bear.

Against the backdrop of the setting sun, the little town is cuter than its postcard. There's a single main road running through the center, lined by sidewalks and old-timey buildings that haven't been updated since the 1800s. No stop lights, but the black top is nice and new. Probably paid for by the bond.

We pass a saloon-style bar with a big wooden sign proclaiming the name: "The Leaky Bucket". It looks like it could be the backdrop for a Western shoot-out scene. There's even a dusty watering trough by the long iron railing that's the perfect place to hitch up some horses.

Across the street is "The Trading Post", a general store fronted by a covered porch filled with rocking chairs. Like the Leaky Bucket, the Trading Post's sign looks vintage.

"This is adorable. Why don't you tell me the town was like this? It's so picturesque. No wonder my mom loved it here."

Teddy shrugs. "The Trading Post was a stop on the Pony Express. Still run by a descendent of the original family. Not much has changed around here."

"Seriously." The whole town has modern touches, but otherwise, it's like time stopped. It would make a pretty good movie set. And that gives me an idea...

Next we roll past a few wide open fields that lead up to a hill with a large stone ledge protruding from the side, like a stage.

"What's that?" I point to the stage.

"Daisy wanted that built. Some sort of outdoor Shakespeare-in-the-park idea she had. We built it out, and then the night the play was supposed to be performed, we had a freak thunderstorm, and we had to relocate inside. And that was that."

"Hmmm." The stage isn't huge, but there's plenty of space in the fields around it. I talked to the triplets about some ways to fundraise money and write for grants, but now I'm getting even more ideas. I know I'm healing because my brain is moving fast again.

The town meeting is in an old adobe building that Teddy tells me used to be a school before it was converted to a recreation center. There's a long hall filled with seats, facing a stage. Under the scent of cleaning fluid, the building smells old.

Teddy guides me inside with a hand on my back, nodding to the townspeople we pass. Everyone recognizes him, and they look at me curiously. I want to wave and greet them, but I've got the hoodie pulled over my hair and half my face. I'm supposed to be in disguise, so I let Teddy hustle me to the front.

The Bad Bear brothers have taken over the first row. Everest is at the end, overflowing from his seat, which creaks under his massive bulk. Even Matthias and the gangly teens look like they've been seated at the kiddie table. I've been around werebears so long, human-sized things look tiny.

Teddy lowers himself carefully into his seat and stretches his arm around me. Across the way, to the far right in front of the stage, stands Darius in a suit. He gives Teddy a nod and me a wink.

Teddy's chest rumbles with a growl. I lean in, and I put a hand on his knee to distract him. "Thank you for letting me come."

He covers my hand with his, but none of the tension seeps out of his shoulders.

Canyon is sitting on my left. "There's the mayor." He points to the white-haired lady slowly ascending the stage.

"Daisy, right?" I whisper back.

"Yep." He chuckles. "She looks the part, doesn't she?"

Daisy is wearing a floral print dress and a big headband affixed with fake flowers. It looks like daisies are sprouting all over her head. On her feet are wedge flip flops with a big single daisy glued to each top. I love that she's stuck with the theme.

Daisy shuffles to the podium. She wobbles a little when stepping onto the raised platform that will help her reach the microphone. I hold my breath, but she makes it.

By the time she's finished adjusting the mic, the room has quieted.

"Welcome to this emergency forum for the town of Bad Bear. As you know, we're in a bit of a kerfuffle."

"That's an understatement," someone shouts from the back.

Daisy looks down her nose at the man in a dusty Stetson who interrupted. "I heard that, Abraham Benson. I see you haven't changed since I taught you math in middle school. And didn't your mother teach you to take off your hat in polite company?"

"Yes ma'am," he mumbles and whips the hat off.

"That's Abe," Canyon whispers. "He owns the Leaky Bucket. Only Daisy can call him 'Abraham.'"

"She taught school?" I whisper back.

"Seventh grade math for thirty years. If she was a bear, she'd still be hibernating."

Daisy is still addressing Abe. "I'll thank you for settling down now. And if someone starts throwing spitballs, I'll know it was you."

Abe leans back in his chair with a creak. "She always knew," he mutters to the people around him, and they nod in commiseration.

"As I said, we're in a bit of a mess, money wise. Fortunately, Mr. Medvedev is here to help us sort everything out. You know him as Darius, one of the "Terrible Twins.""

I twist to look up at Teddy. "Terrible Twins," I mouth. Teddy rolls his eyes.

"Oh, yes," Canyon says gleefully. "Teddy and Darius were the OG Bad Bears."

"Shhh," Hutch says.

On stage, Daisy has gone on to describe the "kerfuffle" as a "bit of a predicament" and introduce Darius as CEO of Medvedev Enterprises. Apparently his company completed successful real estate projects in Albuquerque and Santa Fe, investing in areas in need of housing and grocery stores, replacing food deserts with mixed use buildings that have shops, townhouses, sidewalks and tastefully laid out landscaping to lure people to live there happily ever after.

At least, according to Daisy, who sounds like she's reading from a Medvedev Enterprises brochure. The more she gushes over Darius, the more rigid Teddy's thigh muscles get.

"Please welcome Darius Medvedev," Daisy finishes, and people clap politely.

Darius ascends the stage with a politician's smile. He's removed his suit jacket and unbuttoned his collar, balancing the slick CEO look with a more relaxed, down-to-earth facade. He kisses Daisy's cheeks and helps her down the steps to her seat before bounding up to the microphone.

"Hello, good citizens of Bad Bear. First of all, I'd like to confess," Darius says, "It was me who stole Old Man Luther's boxers off his clothesline and ran them up the flagpole my junior year."

"I knew it!" a stooped man in the back, presumably Old Man Luther, creaks.

From her seat, Daisy shakes a finger at Darius.

Darius ducks his head in mock shame, his hair flops into his face, making him look like a boy a decade younger.

"I have a store credit at the Trading Post with your name on it, Mr. Luther, sir."

"That'll do," Old Man Luther subsides.

The smile slips away from Darius' face. "But seriously folks, I have to apologize. When I first approached the town council with the idea to issue a bond, I thought it was the answer to our problems. And it's my fault the Adalwulf hedge fund took an interest in investing in us. I flew out to New York and spoke to the Adalwulfs personally. They're great people, a family firm, but they run a business and need a return on investment like anyone else. But fortunately," he raises his voice, "they're willing to give us a little more time to make good on our debts. Especially when I showed them all the interest there is in developing the land and building high quality housing and shops that will showcase the beauty of our mountain."

From there, Darius launches into his spiel. His presentation is clean and flashy. With the help of some stage hands, who look like teens recruited from the high school theater department, he sets up a few tripod stands. Each stand displays a presentation board that helps outline his project. There's not much text, but a lot of pictures of happy looking people sitting on benches or walking their dogs, all in front of town houses built against the backdrop of Bad Bear's mountain summit. From the look of it, the real estate development will solve the town's debt problem, operate on zero net carbon emissions, and probably lower cancer rates and heart disease too.

"Are people going to fall for this?" I whisper to Canyon, who shrugs.

"It looks pretty good."

Sure, it looks pretty. But what sort of infrastructure will it take to support so many new homes? And if the influx of new people brings more shops, will chain stores take over and drive the quaint local shops out of business?

I bite my lip. I'm not going to say anything until I'm sure it's warranted.

Turns out, Teddy has the devil's advocate position covered.

Darius turns away from his presentation with hands splayed and asks, "Any questions?"

Teddy rises and stands with his thumbs hitched in his jeans. "I have a few."

"Go right ahead." Darius waves a hand as if giving Teddy the floor. There's a big ole smile on his face, but the gesture is a bit sarcastic.

Teddy calls his twin's bluff and vaults onto the stage, advancing with a big-toothed smile. "Don't mind if I do." He swipes the mic and shoulders Darius out of the way. "I'm Teddy," he says, and when some feedback screeches, he doesn't blink an eye. "I'd like to remind you of what Darius himself said in the beginning of his talk. He's part of the reason we're in this mess. And I don't think we can rely on him to get us out of it."

~

TEDDY

A sea of faces stare up at me when I shield my eyes. The lights on stage are on full blast. Figures Darius would want the full spotlight treatment. He always did like drama in high school.

If he wants drama, I'll give it to him. I'm taking him down tonight. Our last fight was a draw, but this time, we'll see who's the last man standing.

I clear my throat and continue. "Yeah, this presentation looks nice. But so did the idea of a bond solving all our trouble. Ask yourself if a man who's cozy with the hedge fund vultures really has our best interest at heart."

"That's a good point," Old Man Luther says.

"Hear, hear," calls Canyon. Darius glares at him.

"I think this new development looks pretty." I pace the stage, waving to the placard display of happy people in front of their happy housing. "But with it will come infrastructure costs. How much more will we have to spend on roads and sewer systems?" I pause to let my point land. I need to break this down, so everyone can understand. "I'm not saying it can't be done. Lots of suburbs run into this problem, and they simply sell off more land to pay for past construction. The result? Constant sprawl and more debt. That's right, folks, more debt. New houses need new infrastructure, and we'll have to pay for it. To pay for it, we'll need to issue another bond. We'll be in the same situation all over again."

"That's a good point," someone shouts from the back.

Darius rubs sweat from his forehead. The hot lights aren't doing him any favors right now. "The new housing will provide taxes to pay—"

"It won't be enough," I interrupt. Darius can project as well as any actor who played Hamlet, but I still have the mic. "Besides, who's going to buy our bonds with an almost default on our books?"

Darius blinks at me. I flash my fangs. *That's right, brother. You're not the only one who understands munis. I don't need a fancy MBA to talk business.*

"I have the hedge fund's assurance that they wouldn't do that. They would extend good terms—"

"So then we'll be in debt with them forever." I'm face to face with Darius now. It's like looking in a mirror of a metrosexual version of myself, a version who wears hair gel and cologne. "I'd appreciate it if you'd use your in with the hedge fund to get another meeting with them. Tell them to fuck off." I go to hand the mic back to Darius, and he reaches for it. At the last second, I let it drop.

"Ooh," a few smartasses in the front row chorus. Someone else starts clapping. Lana. I nod to her.

"Your move," I mouth at Darius.

"Well, I about heard enough," the owner of the Leaky Bucket, Abe, stands and hitches up his pants. "And all I got to say is, if the development is so bad, then what's your idea?" He turns in a slow circle to address everyone around him. "Teddy told us all the reasons why we shouldn't take Darius' offer. But what's the alternative? Shut down all services? Austerity measures? That's what the hedge fund proposed when we started missing payments. They want their money first. And don't forget, we put up the new county clinic as collateral. The fund will seize it, and folks will have to go all the way down to Santa Fe for medical care."

That was surprisingly well put for Abe. I narrow my eyes at Darius, who raises his brows back at me. Apparently he planned his moves ahead.

"I say we vote for the condos," Abe declares.

A few rows over, a lanky woman in a buckskin vest leans back in her seat. "I say you go back to Old Virginny where your family came from!"

Lana's mouth has rounded to a little 'o'. With my shifter hearing, I catch Canyon's murmured explanation. "That's Terri. She owns the Trading Post across the street from the Leaky Bucket. She and Abe hate each other. Long story."

Abe whirls on the woman. "You shut your mouth, Terri. My great, great grandaddy settled here before yours! He had just as much a right to be here—"

"And after his well ran dry, he stole from ours!" Terri's

cowboy boots hit the floor with a thud. Any second now, she and Abe will be in each other's faces, screaming their heads off. Their feud runs deep.

Darius and I exchange glances, rolling our eyes. He's picked up the mic, but when I reach for it, he blocks me. We tussle, sending reverb squealing around the big space. Half the crowd shudders and covers their ears. The other half are egging Abe and Terri on. Old Man Luther is also on his feet, telling anyone who will listen about the evils of boxer-stealing brothers, hedge funds, and the Nixon presidency.

Everyone's riled up, except for Daisy, who has her hearing aids out and seems to be taking a little nap. Beside her, her granddaughter, a twenty something with a matching daisy headband, is trying to wake her.

"She's got an idea!" Hutch jumps onto stage and points to Lana. She shakes her head, but Canyon urges her to her feet. Between him and Bern, they usher her on stage.

"No." I block her from moving to the podium, but Darius grabs my arm.

"Theodore, let her be. I want to hear what she has to say."

I growl at him, but the distraction allows Hutch to slip Lana by me. Before I know it, Lana is on the podium, and Darius is beside her.

"Hello," she says to him with a sweet smile, motioning to the mic. "May I have that?"

"Let her talk," Bern shouts. With a shark's smile, Darius hands Lana the mic. People settle into their seats. Abe and Terri are still arguing loudly, but Everest rises from his seat on the end of the row and prowls over to them. He doesn't say anything to settle them down, but he doesn't have to. He just looms menacingly, and Terri and Abe shut their mouths and sit down.

"Hello, everyone, I'm Lana L— um, that is, a friend of Teddy's." She gulps and glances back at me. I nod to her. This is important to her. She wanted to help. The least I can do is let her.

Then I'll whisk her off stage to a secluded location and keep her there, tied to my bed until Bentley is no longer a threat.

"I have some ideas to catch up on the bond payments and also to pay the debt off. For good." Lana clears her throat. "First things first. The hedge fund can't force austerity measures or seize assets without a court order, so you have time. And I bet they'd much rather negotiate with you to get the money."

"How do we pay them?" Abe shouts. "There's no money."

"There are several ways! First of all, I saw a beautiful open space on my way here. There's a new music festival starting up, and they're looking for a venue. This place is exactly what the organizer is looking for. It wouldn't take much to persuade them to come here. "

"How?" This from Terri, who has her arms crossed in front of her, just like Abe.

"I'm friends with Anara," she says simply, naming a huge pop star. "She got her start in a small town like this and wants to give back to budding artists on her label. She'll headline."

The name Anara has people sitting up and taking notice.

"I like Anara," says Terri. "Good music."

Abe harrumphs. "What's that going to cost us?"

"Oh, you won't be paying her to sing. She's investing in the event. She'll pay you for the space. The first year, you'll need to roll the payment into building out the venue, adding public bathrooms, etc. But that won't be too costly.

And it will support other projects, like an arts festival or other music events. Artists might come here instead of performing in Kit Carson Park in Taos. Move over Coachella!" She pumps her fist into the air. Her enthusiasm is contagious. People murmur to each other, considering the idea. "The event will require staff, some of which they'd hire locally. So more jobs, especially for students who loved theater in high school." She grins at the stage hands, who look ready to cheer. "And it'll bring in tourists, which means more traffic for local shops." This comment has Abe and Terri settling back in their seats with satisfied smiles.

"Most attendees will spend the night off-mountain, but there could be good business in local rentals. The town could set up an authorized website to take bookings for homestays and vacation rentals. Like Airbnb, but the town verifies the home and gets a cut."

"I could make the website," Hutch offers. More people are nodding. Lana's winning them over.

"By the way, I agree with Darius. Somewhat. To completely pay off the bond, I think you could consider building housing. But not necessarily what Medvedev Enterprises offers. You could put the word out for bids, and stipulate the project is sustainable and preserves designated wild areas. The winning development would invest in their own roads and the additional sewage. And you can change the town's bylaws to support local business and discourage big box stores."

"But what about the next bond payments?" Darius calls loud enough to be heard over everyone's murmuring. "The town needs immediate cash."

Lana cocks her head to the side. Her hood has fallen back, and the pink tips of her hair are peeking out. "There are lots of ways to leverage what you already have to earn more. For example, my Uncle Benny scouts for new locations for movies. I bet this place would be perfect for it. New Mexico is fast becoming a top place to film."

"I think all of this sounds wonderful," Daisy says. Her granddaughter has helped her up the steps. "We'll have to move fast. Summer is around the corner."

"I'll call my contacts!" Lana says. "As soon as I get my phone fixed. And I can invite Anara here to scout the place. If everything looks good, she'll make the announcement right away. She can film it right on Main Street."

Canyon hops back on stage and leans into the mike. "I also…uh… know someone who owns a designer clothing business. She'd like to film a few commercials here, for starters." He and Lana exchange smiles.

"Well, that will certainly put Bad Bear on the map," Daisy says. "Thank you, dear, for getting the word out."

Lana beams. "The press will be all over it! Trust me, we'll have no problem letting the whole world know."

I should have seen it coming, but I was transfixed by Lana's brilliance. Suddenly the reality of what she's suggesting hits me. I rock back onto my heels, the breath gusting out of me like I caught a fist in the solar plexus.

Cameras. Film crews. Paparazzi.

Darius leans close. "Seriously, this is your girl's idea? This is Tiffany all over again."

Cold washes over me. He's right, and he's wrong.

This isn't Tiffany all over again.

It's much, much worse.

12

Lana

That went well. At least, I hope it did. Public speaking isn't my favorite, but I can put on a good show. My cheeks hurt from smiling, but I wave and thank everyone before stepping off the podium and handing Daisy the mic.

Daisy squeezes my arm as she passes. "Well, nothing's set in stone, but it looks like we have a few options after all. Let's all give a big hand to Lana for her ideas!" There are a few stomps and cheers among the golf claps, mostly from the triplets in the front row, but it warms my heart.

A shadow falls over me. Teddy. "This way." He puts a hand on my back to guide me into the wings. We pass Darius, who's smirking. I frown at him.

"That was great!" Canyon pops up next to me. "You did it! You saved the town! Do you really know Anara?"

"Canyon." Teddy's voice is tense. "Get back to your seat."

The teen stops short when he sees Teddy's face. His Adam's apple bobs, and he disappears to the front.

My eyes still haven't adjusted from the bright lights out

front, but there's tension in Teddy's stance. "Teddy? What's wrong?"

"It's nothing." HIs voice is clipped. He grabs my hand and takes me further backstage, into a green room filled with pieces of wood, a few wigs, and an old upright piano.

When I get a look at his grim expression, my whole body turns cold.

I pull my hand out of his grip. "It's not nothing. You're upset."

"We'll talk about it later."

Back on stage, Daisy is calling for the town to vote yea or nay on Darius' proposition.

I swallow, my hand on my chest. "You need to go. Get your vote in."

Teddy curses. "Stay here. I'll be back soon. Don't go anywhere, don't show your face. And keep your hair covered."

I pull up the hood. Something's very wrong. "I'm sorry, I shouldn't have gotten on stage. I thought I was helping. It all happened so fast—"

With another curse, Teddy whirls and tugs me close. He squeezes me tight and kisses my forehead. "Wait here for me. Stay safe. I'll be right back."

I touch the place he kissed as he leaves. That didn't feel like a Viking hug. It felt like goodbye.

LANA

I wait in the green room, biting my lip and watching for Teddy to reappear when a young woman in a floral headband like Daisy's ventures in.

"Excuse me, are you Lana Langmeyer?"

"Yes?" If I sound uncertain, it's because I'm not sure I

should confess my identity. That's probably why Teddy's so upset. I shouldn't have gotten on stage in front of everyone—I just got caught up in the moment.

"I hoped it was you! I'm not a resident, so I'm not voting, and I figured I could catch you back here. I'm a huge, huge fan of GoddessWear." She splays her hands, showing off the fitted dress that hugs her curves and soft belly. The design is my most popular.

"I can see that. You look wonderful. The lavender suits you."

"Thank you!" She touches her hair and grimaces, pulling off her head band. "I know it clashes with the fake flowers. My grandma likes to see me in daisies."

"I think it's adorable. What's your name?"

"Maisy. Well, it's Daisy, but everyone calls me Maisy. OMG," she says, putting her hands to her pink cheeks. "I can't believe I'm really talking to you! I wasn't sure it was you, but then I saw Instagram. I'm a huge fan of your company."

"That's wonderful…" My stomach lurches as I realize what she said. "But what did you see on Instagram?"

"Oh!" Maisy holds up her phone. "Someone posted and tagged you."

Icicles zing up my spine. Someone recorded my impromptu presentation. There I am, on stage, my pink hair on full display. The comment reads: "At a town meeting, and this chick looks just like Lana. @GoddessLana, is this you?" Because I'm tagged, a bunch of people have commented. "Gurl, luv the hair!" Someone else tagged Anara, and now her fans are commenting. There's over a thousand likes already.

"Oh no…" I tighten the hood around my hair, as if that'll help. "Can you take this down? I'm not supposed to be here."

"No, sorry, I didn't post it."

"Crap." I sway on my feet and close my eyes.

"Is that bad? Are you in hiding?"

Maisy sounds concerned, so I open my eyes and try to force a smile. I feel ill.

"Sort of. It's not good if people know I'm here." Or alive at all. "Is there a back door to this place?" I look around, ready to rush out right now. I won't, of course, I'll wait for Teddy.

"Yes, it's back that way."

"Thank you. Is the vote almost done?"

"It's over," Teddy says from the door, and I run to him. "We need to be going."

I wave to Maisy, trying to act normal. "It was nice to meet you."

"Come on." Teddy hustles me to the back. We pass Darius, who's stacking the placards of his presentation against the wall.

"Bye, Lana," he calls. I don't like his tone of voice.

"What happened?" I ask Teddy. "Did the vote pass?"

"No. Your presentation did its job. Enough people were convinced they had other options and didn't need to jump on Darius' scheme."

I gulp. That's good, right? Teddy looks like he wants to punch something.

"Teddy," I clutch his arm. "Daisy's granddaughter showed me her phone. Someone recorded me and put it on Instagram. I'm so sorry."

"It's not your fault, babygirl." A little of his Teddy gentleness slips into his otherwise strained voice. "I got the alert from my Army buddies–they're monitoring your name, and they can get the video down."

"Is there a chance the assassin didn't see it?"

"We'll figure that out. Right now, I need to get you to safety."

~

Safety turns out to be yet another cabin deep in the woods. This one is by a waterfall.

"This is Matthias's place. It should be secure."

I sink onto the couch. Teddy paces back and forth. He was silent the whole ride here.

Something's really wrong.

"You'll be safe here." He heads for the door.

"Where are you going?"

"I need to call my friends back and talk with Matthias about something."

I rise, wringing my hands. "Teddy, please talk to me. You're upset, I can tell."

He stops with his hand on the doorknob, his head dropping.

"I'm sorry I got on stage," I say. "I was just trying to help."

"Yeah. Help." He rubs his eyes. "Did you talk out your plan beforehand with Hutch and Canyon?"

"We talked about some of it. My uncle Benny, filming the commercial. The concert idea I got when we drove past the festival site."

"I see."

"Did I do something wrong?"

He still hasn't turned around to look at me. "This isn't going to work."

"What?"

"You're famous.

"Not that famous."

"Someone recognized you right away. And all your

ideas to raise money—they all involve tons of press and new traffic to the mountain. You're supposed to be dead, Lana. You can't hook up your phone and start calling people."

"Crap," I whisper. "I didn't think."

"No, the problem is, you did think. You thought like a human."

I flinch.

Teddy continues, "Did you really think that bringing the press and a bunch of cameras onto the mountain would solve our problems?"

"I thought it would help."

"I told you a secret. And the first thing you do is get up on stage and tell everyone how you're going to bring tons of media attention to our mountain. Our privacy means more to us than anything. We can't have word getting out about us. We need to hide. That means no cameras and no crowds."

I blink rapidly, my eyes burning. "I can fix it," I plead. "Tell me what I can do to make it right, and I'll do it."

"No. Damage is done. Daisy and the others can't wait to get a bunch of tourists up here. You humans are all the same." His face is gone cold. He's looking at me like he looks at Darius—like I betrayed him.

He turns back to the door.

"Where are you going?" My voice rises into shrill territory.

"I need some air. You need to stay here."

My stomach twists. "Teddy, please." I don't want him to leave. It's less about my safety and more that I feel like I'm losing him. He's really upset.

"I need to figure out what I'm going to do. Don't blame yourself, Lana."

"It's my fault." I blink, looking up at the ceiling to force my tears to roll back where they came. "I didn't mean to do this."

"I know. Maybe it's better that we figure this out now."

"So what are you saying?"

"This isn't going to work. You're human. I'm a were-bear. We live in different worlds."

I press a hand to my sternum, where my heart feels like it's bleeding out in my chest.

I finally found a family. Too bad I'm the wrong species.

This time when he pulls the door open, I don't stop him. He murmurs something under his breath that sounds like, "I shouldn't have made this mistake again."

~

Teddy

I feel like I'm moving underwater. My senses are dulled, muted. Inside my chest, my bear gnashes and roars.

I ignore him.

"There's still time," Matthias says. We're standing behind the ATV between the waterfall and the cabin. I've always loved the sound of the rushing falls. It's peaceful, musical. But tonight, I hear nothing.

When Tiffany betrayed me, it didn't hurt like this. But it's my fault for trusting a human again.

"I still have the leech standing by. You can take her and mindwipe her." Matthias pauses, waiting for my answer. After a minute of silence, he clears his throat. "You can still help her, Teddy. Just because she won't remember you, doesn't mean you'll forget. You can still hunt down her stepbrother, make sure he doesn't hurt her."

"Yeah," I rasp. But she'll lose her memories of this time on the mountain. Her memories of the hike to scatter her parent's ashes. She won't remember Bentley trying to kill her, which might be a blessing. But she won't remember Bad Bear Mountain or my brothers. Or me.

My bear bellows, trying to get out. But for once, I'm in control.

Matthias waits patiently. I remember years ago when we had this same conversation. I was a mess. I screamed at him—in denial. It took both him and Darius to calm me down.

Now I'm cold. All my emotion is stuffed down deep inside me, with my raging bear. "If we do this...if we mindwipe her... can you promise me it won't mess her up? She'll still be able to run her company and lead a long life?"

"There's no guarantees, but there's a good chance she'll be fine." He pauses. "Tiffany adjusted. It took awhile, but we had more memories to wipe. Months' worth. With Lana, we'll only have to mindwipe the past few days."

Has it only been a few days? It feels like I've known Lana forever. In some ways, I have—I've been waiting for her my whole life.

Cutting Lana out of my life will be like chopping off a limb. Hell, I might as well tear out my own heart.

But it's the only way. I need to keep my family safe. The triplets will hate me for doing this to Lana, but they'll understand. Eventually.

"I guess if we're going to mindwipe her, it's better to do it now than wait any longer." My chest seizes like my heart is withering away.

I expect Matthias to tell me it'll be a kindness, but he isn't listening. He's looking back at the cabin, where the cabin door has creaked open. "Lana."

I whirl.

"Teddy?" Her dark skin is ashen. "What are you talking about? What do you mean by *mindwipe* me?"

13

Lana

I'm going to puke.

Teddy's guilty gaze flies to my face.

Matthias clears his throat. "I can explain."

"No." Teddy puts a hand on his brother's shoulder. "I'll do it." His voice is leaden. He sounds a million years old.

He sucks in a breath and then says quickly, as if he's ripping off a bandage, "A mindwipe is something a vampire can do. The leeches—vampires—can remove someone's memories. We do it when a human has found out about us, and we need them to forget. The vampire can take away their memories, so the human doesn't remember about shifters anymore."

Humans.

Shifters.

So stark, so black and white. I thought Teddy and I had a connection. I thought we were mates, and it was fate. I thought I found a family. But here he is talking like he's one species, and I'm another. It's worse than having a rich, white stepfather. Way worse.

"You would do that to me?" I ask. "Make me forget you? Us?"

Matthias looks from me to Teddy and back again. "I'll let you guys talk this out. He gives me a nod and disappears into his cabin.

Teddy's still turned away from me, his shoulder stiff. "It might be for the best."

I choke. "You think that? You think that it would be for the best if this had never happened? If I never found out who you are? If we'd never been together?"

Matthias talked about true mates, and I got my hopes up. But obviously I'm not Teddy's one and only. Because right now he's trying to throw me away like trash.

And I'm not going to let him. I raise my chin. "Fine. Do it."

"What?" Teddy's head comes up. "Babygirl—"

"No, you don't get to call me that anymore. I'm going to forget all about you, remember? I want it done." The air in my lungs has turned into daggers. Each breath is painful. "I thought we had something good. I felt it in me. I thought I was going to be a part of your family."

"Lana—" He puts a hand on my arm, and I shake him off. No more Viking cuddles. If he puts his arms around me, I'm going to fall apart.

"You know what Teddy? You're right. Your secret is too important. If this will help you, if this will keep your family safe, then I want it done." I whirl and rap on the cabin door. "Matthias? I'd like to go now."

Matthias pads out, his face expressionless. I feel endlessly tired. "I'd like to go now. I'm volunteering to do this mindwipe thing. Can we make a stop to pick up my bag with all my things?"

"Lana." Teddy's at my side. I hold up a hand and don't look at him. "No, I don't want to talk to you anymore. I don't want to see you. If this relationship is ending, it's ending on my terms." I turn to Matthias and say words I'd never thought I'd say. "Take me to the vampire."

Matthias peers at me, and I get the feeling he's seeing more than my squared shoulders and the tears tracking down my face. "You sure about this?"

"I'm sure. But I want to ride with you and not with him." I've put my back to Teddy, making it clear I'm talking to Matthias now. If anyone's going to take me to get this procedure done, it's going to be him.

"Lana," Teddy growls. "I don't want it to end like this."

"Too bad. You made your choice, and now I've made mine." I look at Matthias and not him. "I want to go now."

∼

LANA

Matthias takes me down the mountain in the ATV. We make a stop at the triplet's cabin for my bag. No one seems to be home, but Matthias leaves me in my seat while he runs in to grab my stuff, just in case. He and I agree, If the Terrible Threes get wind of what I'm about to do, this will get messier than it already is. Best case, they'll make a fuss. Worst case, they'll have Everest kidnap me in an attempt to *rescue* me from my fate. I sit tense in the ATV, waiting for shouts of outrage, half expecting Hutch and Canyon to burst out of the cabin, shouting for Bern to get the chopper, so I can escape.

But that doesn't happen. Matthias gets in and gets out, returning to my side with my pink backpack in hand. The fabric glows in the dark, but the sight doesn't cheer me as it typically would. I'm completely drained of cheer. Trying to think of a positive spin on the situation just makes me feel tired.

Dully, I wonder how the mindwipe works exactly.

Matthias lets the silence stretch between us as the ATV bounces down the trail between the dark rows of trees.

I force myself to open my mouth and ask some questions. "How long is the drive?"

"A few hours."

I sink into the seat. Only a few hours to hold onto my memories of Teddy. The good ones. "Will it hurt?"

"No."

"How do you know? Have you ever been mindwiped?"

"No, Lana. I've never been mindwiped. But it doesn't hurt. It's like being hypnotized. It'll be just like falling asleep."

That's fitting. I'll fall asleep, and everything I've experienced will be like a dream. Will I wake up well rested or scared and confused, like I had a nightmare? I guess it doesn't matter.

Matthias is still talking. His voice is smooth and even, like a professor's, and I tune him out until he stops and glances over at me.

I bob my head as if I agree to whatever he's said.

"You'll be okay, Lana."

"Uh huh." My voice sounds dead.

We both know that's a lie.

The ATV rolls out of the forest and into a private parking lot that looks a lot like the one where my rental SUV was parked before it exploded. "This is me." He motions to a red sports car. If I was in a good mood, I would tease him about buying a flashy doctor car, but I'm not, so I dismount and walk over to the passenger side, feeling numb.

Beside the car is a big silver Mercedes SUV. A light goes on inside, revealing a big blond guy. I catch my breath for a second, thinking it's Teddy, but no, it's Darius. I can tell by the way he holds himself as he exits the car. He's barefoot and no longer in his suit, but stripped down to an undershirt and slacks.

"Darius," Matthias greets him. "You went for a run?"

"Just got back and changed," Darius confirms. His eyes flash silver when they light on me. "What's going on?"

"I'm going to be mindwiped," I tell him. "Teddy and I broke up."

Darius narrows his eyes.

Matthias opens the car door for me, and I slide inside. I don't want to explain anything more than I already have.

Matthias and Darius confer a moment in muffled voices. I don't even try to listen in. Soon enough, the driver's side opens, but to my surprise, it's not Matthias but Darius who slides in.

Matthias taps on my window. "Darius wants to drive you. Is that okay?"

"Sure," I say. What does it matter?

Darius adjusts the rear view window. "There are a few things I want to tell you on the way there."

I clutch my bag to my chest and turn my head to look out the window. "Whatever." I sound like a surly teenager for the first time in my life.

Darius puts the car in gear, and it purrs from its parking spot. Matthias stands with his hands in his pockets, watching us go. I probably should have said goodbye. But it's not like I'm not going to remember him or anyone else anyway.

∽

Teddy

What. In the hell. Was I thinking?

How could I, for even one minute, consider erasing Lana's memories of me?

The moment she leaves, it's like my heart left my chest. No, more like every organ left my body. I'm left a pile of dry bones, with nothing to give me life.

I try to stagger to the cabin but find myself on my knees in the dirt. My legs don't even work.

"Lana." I try to say her name, but it comes out as raspy cough. Like my mouth is full of dirt. Too dry to even form a word. "Lana," I try again with no greater success.

What have I done?

Can this really be the answer? If this was right, why would it feel so wrong? Not just wrong—horribly, horribly off.

But Matthias thought it was right. So did Darius.

They had to intervene with Tiffany, too.

Am I just unable to see what has to be done here? Am I blinded by lust for the sweet human?

Mate! my bear roars.

And that's when real fear sets in. Because if my bear is right–if Lana is our mate–I just fucked myself beyond all fuckery.

Shifters who find a mate and don't claim her turn feral.

I just signed my own death warrant in order to save the mountain.

And honestly–I don't even care about death. Because dying is nothing compared to the pain of knowing I hurt Lana. Knowing the last thing she'll remember of me– although not for long now–will be my total betrayal.

LANA

There's a boulder in my throat, threatening to choke

me. I focus on taking deep breaths, so I don't have to ride next to Darius with tears streaming down my face. When we pass the Bad Bear Mountain sign, I close my eyes, so I don't have to see the painted bears romping across the faded wood.

"So what happened?" Darius asks, his voice casual like he's asking about the weather.

I grip my bag tighter. "Teddy says we're from different worlds."

"He's right, you know. You are," Darius says, and I briefly contemplate throwing my bag at his head. I don't want to ride the whole way with Darius saying, "I told you so." I don't want to look at him right now because he looks so much like Teddy. A business-minded, anal retentive version of Teddy, but Teddy all the same. Darius even has let his beard grow out a little messier, probably for the town meeting.

Darius lets a few miles of road pass before saying,"You know, the last time Teddy was with a human, it went badly."

"Was it Tiffany?"

"Yes, Tiffany. Did Teddy tell you about Tiffany?"

"No. He hasn't told me anything." I'm angry about this Tiffany and whatever she did to screw this up for me. I'm mad at Teddy, and I sure as heck don't love his twin right now, either.

Darius nods. "You need to know about Tiffany."

Great. As if this ride wasn't awful enough, I get to hear about Teddy's ex.

But Darius seems determined. "Teddy was young. They were only eighteen. He thought that she was his mate."

Pain slices through my heart. *Mate.* There's that word again. "So why isn't he with her?" I have to sound like this means nothing to me, like I don't care. In a few hours, I won't remember anything. Will I sense something's missing, like a phantom limb? Will my thoughts stutter over the place where the memories of Teddy were? Or will it be like he never existed at all?

I can't imagine not being able to remember Teddy. Whatever this vampire's going to do to me, I'll probably know deep down that I met someone special and now he's gone.

"Teddy had every intention of spending his life with Tiffany," Darius says. "But the day after Teddy told her our secret, she contacted a reporter with news that she had the story of the century. She reached out to not one but three major newsrooms to see if she could get a bunch of cameras here to break the story."

"Oh," I breathe, stunned.

"Yep. Teddy didn't know any of this. He'd borrowed Ma's truck for a special errand. He'd commissioned an engagement ring from a jeweler all the way down in Albuquerque. While he was planning to propose, Tiffany was going to tell our secret to the world."

The love of Teddy's life planned to betray him after he trusted her with his secrets. No wonder he was twitchy about cameras. "What happened?"

"I overheard her talking to the reporter. She needed proof for the reporter to believe she wasn't making it all up. I grabbed her phone, and Matthias sedated her and made arrangements for the mindwipe. But then we had to tell Teddy. He…didn't take it well."

"I bet." The pain in my chest cavity transforms, softening. I hurt for the young werebear, the hopeful boy that Teddy used to be.

"I was the one who broke the news to him. He didn't believe me until I showed him Tiffany's phone with the record of texts and calls. The only reason Tiffany hadn't told the reporter everything was because she wanted money. Three hundred thousand dollars."

My stomach lurches. She was going to sell Teddy's family out for money? This story is making me ill.

Darius glances in the rearview mirror. "The reporter said Tiffany could get all sorts of money and book deals, but first they needed proof. Tiffany's greed bought us time. Teddy and Matthias took her to the leech."

"Did it work? Did she forget?" I haven't heard a newsbreak about werebears, so it must have.

"Her case was more complicated. She and Teddy had been together for a while. They'd met in high school and were together when Teddy took a few community college courses. The leech had to wipe several months' worth of memories. When Tiffany woke up, she had trouble remembering her own name."

Oh shit. I don't realize I've whimpered aloud until Darius touches my arm.

"It's okay, Lana. It won't be that bad for you. We might have been a little harsh with the mindwipe, too, because we needed to destroy Tiffany's credibility. And it worked. The reporter chalked Tiffany's story up to a delusion, and our secret stayed safe. Thank Fate."

I'm holding my pink bag so tight, my hands cramp. I ease my grip.

"Tiffany recovered after a few months. Matthias kept an eye on her—he'd been a junior EMT, so he had a pretense to check in with her. Last I heard, she took a job driving trucks cross country. She's never come back to this area. No memory of werebears, no trying to get money for the story. But Teddy…A few days after taking Tiffany to be mindwiped, Teddy joined the military. He didn't come back to the mountain for five years."

We drive a few more miles in silence. Me, digesting this. Darius looks grim, like he's reliving the past.

"Is that when you went to college?" I ask, mostly to say something. During the fight between Darius and Teddy, Darius threw out the fact that he'd studied business.

"Someone had to stick around and help Ma," Darius growls. "Teddy was gone. Matthias needed to focus on getting into med school. The Terrible Threes were growing up and getting into everything. Ma didn't have a second to spare. I worked construction and went to school at night. I taught myself to day-trade. Then I went to New York for my MBA. Teddy thinks I abandoned the family, but he did it first." Darius grips the steering wheel tight. If he were Teddy, I'd put a hand on his back to ease the tension in his shoulders.

Maybe this ride is less about me and more about him talking his own stuff out. No better person to hear your secret shame than someone who's about to be mindwiped.

"You did your best," I said. "You both did."

Darius' shoulders soften. "Maybe. I was the one who suggested the town put out a bond. I was young and full of myself. I didn't know what I didn't know. Now the town's in debt, and it's my fault."

"It's okay, Darius. You don't have to explain yourself to me."

"I think I do. You mean something to Teddy."

It's my turn to tense. "No, I really don't."

"He cares about you."

"Maybe. But not enough to make things work. He wants me out of his life. When things got complicated, he let me go."

"Teddy may seem big and tough, but he's a cinnamon roll. Years ago, he put the family at risk. He doesn't want to make the same mistake again."

I riffle through my bag, looking for my chapstick, and come across my broken cell. Matthias has a phone charger coiled in the center console that's a match to mine, so I pull out my phone and plug it in. "What are you trying to say, Darius?"

"I just want you to understand where Teddy is coming from."

"Fine. Thanks, I guess. It's not like I'm going to remember this anyway."

Darius hesitates, like he wants to say more, but I look out the window. We're already on the highway. How much time is left before I forget everything? I should be reviewing all my good memories, but I don't want to arrive at our destination weeping.

Darius keeps glancing in the rear view mirror. Without warning, he cuts his lights and zooms across three lanes of traffic, taking the exit. I fumble for the oh-shit handle, but there isn't one.

"Darius? What are you doing?"

He downshifts, swerving into a U-turn that has me rocking in the seat.

"I think someone's following us."

"What? Where?"

"A black SUV. Back there. We'll take the back roads." He checks the rearview mirror compulsively for the next few minutes and finally relaxes. "Lost them."

My stomach is no longer flipflopping, mostly because I think I left it back on the highway. "Who do you think it is?"

"Some asshole assassin your shithead stepbrother hired."

"Really?" I crane my neck, but the dark road is clear. I should probably be freaking out, but I seem to have reached my freak out quota for the year. Getting murdered by an assassin couldn't feel any worse than I do right now. Getting dumped by my Viking. Finding out he wanted to mindwipe me because I screwed up and suggested we bring publicity to Bad Bear.

God, I trusted the guy! I felt safe with him. But I couldn't have been more endangered.

He tore my heart right in two. And then he sent me off to a vampire.

"How would Bentley even find me?" I ask dully.

Darius scowls at the road ahead of us like it's harboring killers, and he's going to shoot them down with his eyeballs. "Cell phone," he finally barks. "That's how he's tracking you." He rolls down his window, grabs my phone and throws it into the night.

"Hey!" I sit up straight.

"I'll buy you a new one."

I settle back in my seat. "It's okay," I mutter. "I'm going to be mindwiped, right? I'm probably going to forget everyone I've ever known."

"What?" Darius' brow furrows. "That's not how it works. The leech… I mean, the vampire can get down to specific memories. He'll just erase the ones from the past few days."

"Oh. The word *mindwipe* sounds so final."

"Yeah. You'll forget we're werebears, but you'll still remember your life. Matthias told me to take your memories starting at the beginning of the hike. Didn't he or Teddy explain any of this to you?"

"I'm not speaking to Teddy. Matthias might have, but I was pretty upset and wasn't listening."

Darius concentrates on driving for a mile then says quietly, "You love him."

I grimace and hug my bag tighter. "It doesn't matter. In a few hours, I won't even remember him."

"Lana—"

I open my mouth. I just have to say this. "I know Tiffany betrayed him, but I'm not her. I would never do that to him. To any of you. But you don't have to believe me. In a few hours, you'll all be rid of me." I turn away from him and say to the window, "I can't wait."

"Say it again with a little less anger, and then I'll believe you."

I whip my head around to look at Darius. He quirks a brow at me, looking so much like Teddy I want to smack him.

"You love him," he repeats.

"Of course, I love him," I snap.

Darius shakes his head. "Right." The next thing I know, he's slowed Matthias' sports car and whipped us back around.

I grip the seat, digging my nails into the leather.

"Darius! WTF?" I look for a black SUV or any sort of car, following us, but there's nothing. The road is empty.

"This is a mistake," he informs me. "I'm taking you back."

I gape at him.

Darius shifts the car into top gear. "I love my twin. We have our differences. He's a bit quicker than me in a fight, and I'm... better looking."

I snort.

"After the thing with Tiffany, he was hurting. Deep down, I think some part of him blames me because I was the one who found out, and I was the one who told him."

"Darius, what in the heck—"

He holds up a hand, and I shut up in case he takes both hands off the wheel while the car is whipping around a bend. "Listen. What I'm saying is Teddy holds onto things more than most. Since the thing with Tiffany, he hasn't been in a serious relationship. At all. He threw himself into military service and then worked with the Black Wolf pack to get their security business and his helicopter one off the ground. But now he's just wallowing."

My mouth hangs open. I'm trying to wrap my head around what Darius is saying, while bracing myself in the car seat. Two seconds ago, I was headed to a vampire. Now Darius has done a literal 180, and I'm headed back to Teddy?

It feels so right, I think I will cry. But it doesn't matter if Darius thinks mindwiping me is a mistake, Teddy still believes it's the right thing to do.

"He used to be a happy go-lucky guy. To his friends, he still is. But when he feels things, he feels them deep."

"I don't think he's happy around me. He can be a total grump."

"That's because you make him feel. You make him want more. He shut that part of him down a long time ago, and he's grumpy because you're waking it up."

"How would you know? All you guys do is fight."

"I'm his twin," he says simply, as if this explains why he's the expert on Teddy's inner feelings. "And you're his—"

"Don't say it." I raise my hands, palms up, like I'm stopping traffic. Or surrendering. But I really don't want to hear the word *mate*. Matthias hinted something, and it got my hopes up. "If it's true, why would he let me go?"

"Teddy overreacted. He made a mistake. But you're his only hope of rescue, Lana, and I can't let you throw your memories away because my brother's a giant dumbass. You're his mate."

I flinch.

"You are. You know how I know? Tiffany ran to the newsrooms and the cameras to get a second of fame. You're already famous, and you're running to get your mindwiped, so no one can pry the secret out of you. That's love. And I'm not going to let Teddy throw it away."

I open my mouth to say something, I don't know what, but moonlight flashes on an obstacle in the road ahead of us, and I scream, "Look out!"

The sport's car has great brakes. Darius makes good use of them. The tires shriek, and I bounce off the passenger door, but we stop.

There are a bunch of huge black SUVs blocking the road.

"Fuck." Darius shifts the car to reverse and guns it backwards, turning in the road and hurtling back the way we came. "Bentely must've called in the big guns."

Oh right. I almost forgot—my stepbrother's trying to kill me. "More assassins?"

"A whole team of them."

I crane my neck just in time for Darius to brake the car, hard. Another phalanx of black SUVs is blocking the road ahead of us. There's nowhere to go. We're in a canyon of some sort, with hills on either side and no off roads or traces of civilization around. We're trapped.

"Fuck," we both say at the same time. Behind us, the SUV doors have opened, and a few men in black get out.

"Okay, here's the plan." Darius reaches into his pocket and pulls out his phone. "You're going to take this and run into the hills." He punches in a code and hands the cell to me.

"Should I call for help? There's no signal."

"Don't need it. There's a special tracker on there. I just activated it with a distress code." A ghost of a grin flashes over his face. "Teddy programmed it himself. He did it for everyone in the family." He reaches over and grabs my door handle. "On my signal, you run."

"Wait! What about you?"

His smile shows all his teeth. He looks like a shark. "I'm going to be bait.

"But—"

"You're my brother's mate. I'm going to do what it takes to get you out of this alive."

"Darius," I whisper.

"Don't worry, kid." He boops my nose, looking so much like Teddy I want to cry.

"Oh, and I'm taking this." He grabs my glow in the dark backpack. "You ready?"

My chest heaves, like I'm starting to hyperventilate. I gulp and nod.

"On three," Darius says. "I'm going to distract them. And…don't get caught, sweetheart. I need you to send my brothers to rescue me."

14

Teddy

For an hour after Lana leaves, my bear snarls and bellows, fighting to get out. *It's too late*, I tell him. *She's gone.*

She left us. And she did it because I'm an ass. The moment I opened my mouth to tell her about the mind-wipe, I knew it was wrong, but I told her anyway. I didn't trust her, even though she made it clear she'd do anything to help us. She was trying to save us, and in return, I cut her out of my life.

Out of my life but never out of my heart. That would be impossible. Not even a pickaxe could cleave her from that organ.

Not that it matters. I hurt her. Terribly. Irreparably. And right now, she's probably scared and in pain and suffering through her final moments of having me in her life.

Fuck.

She wanted to save our town, but she couldn't save me from myself.

I rub my hands down my face. What the fuck am I'm I doing? How could I have let her go?

An annoying *zzzt zzzt zzzt* comes from my back pocket. I pull out my phone.

"Fuckin' finally," Deke snaps. "I've been trying to reach you. We found Bentley."

"That's good–"

"No, it's not. He and an entire wet work team are on their way to hunt your girl."

I'm on my feet in a shot. "Are you shitting me?"

"No. Is she with you?"

"No." *I let her go.* I don't say the last part. I can't stand to say the truth out loud: I had my mate by my side, and I drove her away. "She's off the mountain. We're separated. She's with Matthias."

"Get him on the phone, and get Lana to a safe location. I'll text you Bentley's last known coordinates. You'll need backup. We're coming down."

I hang up and ring Darius, but the sound of his ringer jangles just outside the door. "What the fuck?"

"Teddy?" Matthias is outside. The ATV rolled up while I was on the phone with Deke. Did he already visit the leech with Lana?

A searing pain lances my heart.

The cabin door bangs open. Hutch, Bern and Canyon appear in a tangle of limbs, fighting to get through the door together.

"I'm going to kill you!" Canyon has his arms outstretched, fingers flexing like they're around my throat. Hutch and Bern are trying to pull him back.

"Where is she?" Canyon shouts. "Lana! We're going to take you to safety!"

"She's not here," Matthias rumbles from behind them.

Axel is beside him, leaning on the ATV, a hand rolled joint in his hand. "Yeah, man. Calm down."

My growl splits the night, and the Terrible Threes settle. I push past them to snarl at Matthias. "Where is she?"

"Darius wanted to take her," Matthias shrugs. "She agreed."

Darius. Fucker.

"We need to get her back."

"The mindwipe is what she wanted."

"What?" Canyon sags in his brothers' arms. "Why?"

"Yeah, why'd she leave?" Hutch pipes up. "We made her a cake."

Everest has appeared next to the ATV holding a homemade three layer cake. White frosting is sliding off the sides. On top is loopy handwriting that looks like it was written by a drunken toddler. It says, 'welcome to the family' with a horrifying brown blob underneath that is supposed to be a bear.

Axel looks from the cake to Everest and back again. "Nailed it."

"I don't know," Hutch says. "I think there was too much water in the frosting–"

"Listen up," I bark. "Lana's in trouble."

Everyone's mouth snaps shut.

"The Black Wolf pack is texting me the enemy's last known location. We need to go."

"Who?" Canyon shrugs off his brothers. "You're not leaving us behind."

"No. I need your help. All of your help." I stare into my assembled brothers' faces, including the triplets. They look so young, but they're family, and I need them. "We need to find Lana and intercept Bentley. We're taking the warbirds. All of them."

My cell starts beeping loudly. So does everyone else's. There's a moment of confusion, while we pull out our phones and stare at the screens.

"What the—" Canyon says.

"The tracker." I clutch my phone. "Darius is sending a distress signal."

"And now we have coordinates," Matthias says.

"Bad bears activate," Hutch says. He looks determined, but there's a questioning lilt to his voice.

"Yes." I grip his shoulder. "Bad bears activate. Now here's what we're going to do."

∼

Lana

My heartbeat echoes in my chest and reverberates through my limbs, but my breathing has slowed in time to Darius' countdown.

"One... Two..."

On three, we both throw our car doors open. I scramble into the brush on the side of the road, my boots scrabbling on the rocky soil.

Darius is shouting something, drawing attention to himself. I put my head down and pelt up the side of the hill. The smell of sage rises as I crush the silvery plants underfoot. I dodge and weave, trying to look for a way to hide. A gap in the hill, some sort of crevice. My hand is molded around Darius' cell phone. I could get to high ground and see if that will allow Teddy to track me better.

At least I'm not in my glow-in-the-dark outfit. I'm still wearing Bern's borrowed hoodie. It's black. That's good. I gather my braids and tuck them into the hood. Between the black hoodie and my jean skirt, hopefully I can blend in to the landscape. Unless the assassins have some sort of night goggles with heat sensors that allow them to see me in the night. Then I'm screwed.

Behind me, my pink backpack glows on the top of the sports car. Darius must have put it there for some reason. He's walking slowly towards the line of SUVs, with his hands in the air.

The SUV's doors are open, spewing a bunch of men in black. The glare of the car's headlights illuminates the long barrels of their black guns.

"Don't shoot," Darius calls. "Don't shoot." He sounds so calm. He's standing in the middle of the road, right in the path of the headlights. The perfect target.

The wet work team raises their guns into place.

Someone's radio crackles. "She's in the hills. We're going after her."

A loud crack of sound bounces off the walls of the canyon. I flinch, flinging myself to the ground, even though the gunshot didn't hit me or land anywhere near me. It must have hit Darius.

Down on the road, there's a roar and a huge dark shape rushes the assassins. Darius, in werebear mode. Bullets crack over and over again. The roaring only gets louder.

I have to do something. Darius is down there fighting or dying, getting shot over and over again. Teddy healed up fast, but that was a cut on his head—oh… and the bullets from the drones. How many bullets can a werebear take before it dies?

On hands and knees, I scramble up the incline. I've got to get to the top. *Come on, Teddy. I need you to rescue me.*

∽

Teddy

The beat of a helicopter's blades sounds like home to me. Ironic that my bear, as big and bad as it is, loves the feel of fresh wind on its face. In the Army, I learned that I loved the sky. Of course, not much can kill a werebear. Maybe that fearlessness makes it even more fun.

Tonight I'm not in the pilot's seat. Bern is there, in his headset. I hang half out the door, searching the terrain. On the other side, Canyon does the same. We're headed to the coordinates Darius' phone tracker sent all of us. If it moves, we'll follow.

So far, it hasn't moved.

I'm coming, brother. Hold on.

Matthias flies another bird with Hutch and Everest. Axel took the third helicopter up towards Taos to pick up as many of the Black Wolf pack as will fit.

If we're lucky, we'll arrive on the scene in time. If we're not—

My chest shakes with my bear's growl. We have to get to Lana in time. There's no other option.

Bern mutters into his headset. "We're almost to the location. Do you have a visual?"

The road is a smooth seam between the hills. Somewhere down in the barren, rocky canyon, Lana is running for her life.

"Tracking signal's down there," Bern reports. "Where are they?"

A bright pink backpack glows in the dark right on top of Matthias's sports car. "There." I point, even though no one can see me. "Pink backpack at two o'clock."

"10-4. Thunderbears are go." Bern angles the helicopter to take us down.

Lana

I'll say this for denim: it's durable and always in style. You can dress it up or down, work all day in it and show up to a party looking like a rockstar. The one thing I don't recommend doing is running in it. It's a small consolation to know your skirt is cute when you're running from a pack of assassins.

I'm still half-running, half-crawling in the vague direction of the hilltop. My knuckles and palms are scraped from the rocks, and sweat sticks the t-shirt to my back.

Downwind, the gunshots and roars have died away. Now and then, the excruciating quiet is punctuated by a random scream or muffled roar. The sound of my own heartbeat thunders.

How long have I been running? My thighs are chafed, and my boobs are bouncing, but it doesn't matter. Adrenaline pushes me up the hill. I don't know if someone's still following me or whether I've gotten away. I might have to run/crawl for miles.

I'm clambering around a boulder when I hear it: the *tak-tak-tak* sound of helicopter blades chopping in the air. I'm high up enough to see the terrain stretching away from me. There's my pink backpack, glowing on Matthias' car on the road below. Moonlight washes over the rocks and scrub trees. Two helicopters hover above the land. One is white. The other behind it is black and harder to see. They're dipping down, sending gusts of dust billowing into the air.

There's a whoop, and a figure leaps out of the white helicopter. I can't see who it is, but whoever they are, they're wearing a kilt. More shouts, and two more figures leap into the air. Lightning flashes in the distance, illuminating three figures hanging from parachutes, floating down.

The sight gives me chills. The helicopters roar overhead. The black one flies over the road, switching on a spotlight that glides over the terrain. More shots ring out as the assassins return fire.

The sound sends me scurrying. I throw myself to the ground, scrambling behind a boulder. Should I climb up or down? My palms skid on the rough rock. My nails are so broken, chipped and splintered, they resemble pink claws. If I'm attacked, I can make like a bear and scratch someone, if I'm not shot first.

I tuck myself into a hiding place and peek out. Down in the road, a parachute has landed. A shirtless, kilted figure strides into the light of the SUV's. It's Canyon. "Yeehaw," he shouts. "The bad bears have arrived."

Bullets spurt and Canyon rolls and rushes at the line of SUVs. Halfway there, his shout turns into a roar. His skinny body morphs into a shaggy shape, still charging. Guns crack over and over. The werebear that is Canyon disappears beyond the SUV's headlights, and I can't see the rest. There's roaring and shooting and random shouts. I grip Darius's cell phone tight and dart from my hiding place. If I get higher, maybe I can see what's going on. There might be assassins hunting me, but I feel a lot safer with a bunch of werebears around.

There's a whine like an angry hornet and bullets strike the rocks around me.

I scream and throw myself down the hill. The assassins have found me, and I don't know what else to do.

Roars blast the bushes around me.

"Teddy," I whimper.

And then he's here. Scooping me up, covering me with his body. "I got you, babygirl," he murmurs.

My ears are ringing, but the bullets have stopped. I press my face into his shoulder, clutching him tight.

"It's okay. It's over." He holds me, carrying me back down the hill. The sounds of battle have died away.

A few bears mill around in the road. The tattered remains of a kilt decorate the blacktop in front of one of the SUVs.

The two choppers have landed, the white one next to the SUVs, the black one further up the road.

As we pass the white one, Bern slides out of the pilot seat with his headset still in place. "The Black Wolf pack is on its way with Axel. They can handle clean up."

"Good," Teddy growls. "Any drones?"

"Not this time," Bern says.

Teddy sets me on a boulder beside the road and starts patting me down. "Are you hurt?"

"No," I murmur. My heart aches at the sight of him. So beautiful. So strong and capable. So…not mine. It makes me want to weep all over again.

He brushes gravel from my knees and fusses over the abrasions on my hands while I sit, drinking in the sight of him. "Lana, I'm so sorry. I fucked up, babygirl. I don't want to lose you. I was so wrong."

My heart stutters.

"Please forgive me. Losing you would be the biggest mistake of my life. I never should have even considered a mindwipe. I know I hurt you, but I swear I will never do it again. Not ever."

My lips tremble. "You did hurt me."

"I got scared. I was afraid I'd endangered the mountain and my kind, and I completely lost sight of what I know." He holds my gaze. "That you're good. You're kind. You'd never intentionally hurt us. And most of all–that I can't live without you."

My breath leaves my chest in a whoosh.

"Y-you can't?"

He shakes his head, his grey eyes full of mourning. "Not even for an hour, babygirl."

I wrap my arms around his neck. "I can't live an hour without you, either," I declare.

Teddy holds me so tight, I can't breathe, and I absorb all his passion. His strength. His caring.

"Did we get them all?" Canyon steps out from behind an SUV, buck naked. I avert my eyes.

"Put some clothes on," Teddy barks. Canyon turns and marches back where he came from with a snicker.

"All good over here," Hutch calls from somewhere on our left. "Teddy, you're going to want to see this."

Teddy lets out a sound that's less an angry growl and more a frustrated rumble. He scoops me up and carries me in the direction of Hutch's voice. It's as if he's unwilling to be away from me for more than a second.

There's a furry bulk lying beside the road. A shirtless Hutch is kneeling next to it. The teen must not have taken bear form or figured out a way to keep his kilt intact, because he's wearing it.

"Oh no," I gasp. "Is that—?"

"Darius," Teddy confirms. I whimper, pressing a hand over my mouth. "He said he'd create a diversion. They must have shot him multiple times." I can't bring myself to ask if he's dead.

The bear's body shrinks, the fur disappearing until a tall Viking lays splayed out on the ground.

Teddy sets me down and strides forward. He pulls off his jacket and tosses it over Darius's crotch. Darius wakes up and jackknifes in half to catch the jacket a second before it hits him.

"Cover yourself up," Teddy orders.

"Took you long enough to get here, fucker," Darius

retorts. "What were you doing, moping on the mountain while I was giving my all to protect your mate?"

My breath catches. Has Teddy accepted that I'm his mate?

"That's right." Teddy pulls me into his side. "She's my mate and don't you forget it."

She's my mate. I lean into him and focus on Darius. "Are you okay?" His pale skin is streaked with blood, but I don't know if it's his or the assassins'.

His mouth splits into a grin. His beard looks bushier than usual. "All good, sweetheart."

Teddy turns me, so he's between me and his twin. "Quit flirting with my mate."

"I'm not, I swear." Darius chuckles. "I like her, now that I've gotten to know her. I'm sorry I compared her to Tiffany earlier. I was just giving you a hard time."

"You're an asshole," Teddy says.

"Yes," Darius sighs, lying back on the blacktop like he's exhausted. "I am."

He looks so pathetic, I have to say something. I angle my head up to Teddy. "He took a bullet for me. I think possibly several."

"It's no biggie." Darius waves a hand. He glances beyond us and calls, "Matthias, sorry about your car. I'll buy you a new one."

A huge bear with light brown fur sidles up to the car and pauses to examine the bullet riddled doors. The bear that must be a Matthias is somehow still wearing glasses perched on its long snout. It shakes its head mournfully and ambles off into the night.

"You okay, Lana?" Canyon asks, popping out from behind an SUV. He's fashioned some sort of loincloth out of what looks like Hutch's shirt.

"Yes, I'm fine. Thank you for the rescue."

"Teddy," Bern calls. "Can you come here a minute?"

Teddy moves in the direction of his voice, and because we're joined at the hip, I go too.

Behind the SUVs are a bunch of captive assassins. Some are hogtied with gags stuffed in their mouths. Others are lying in a row. Dead or unconscious, I don't want to know. I guess they deserve it.

A polar bear appears, dragging the limp body of an assassin. As it passes, Everest raises a paw and angles it, so a claw points to the sky. I swear he's giving us a thumbs up.

Hutch and Canyon lead us to an SUV with a stack of weapons piled up next to it.

"Look who we found," Bern sounds grim.

In the trunk of the SUV, my stepbrother sits up straight, practically mummified with rope. There's a strip of duct tape over his mouth.

I suck in a breath.

"He says his name is Bentley Dupree, and he'll give us anything if we let him go," Hutch reports.

"I say we give him a running start, and let the bears hunt him." Canyon's grin flashes a mouthful of fangs.

Bentley whimpers behind the duct tape gag. His skin is ghastly white. He looks about twelve seconds from keeling over with fear.

"Seriously, though, he saw us shift," Bern says. "So did the assassins. What are we going to do?"

Teddy motions and Hutch rips the duct tape off Bentley's face.

Bentley's eyes almost roll back in his head. "Bears..." he squeaks in a hoarse whisper. The whites of his eyes flash as he looks around at the ring of brothers. "Bears! Bears!"

Holding Teddy's hand, I stride up to my stepbrother and lean close. "That's right, Bentley. They're Bad Bears."

"Very bad bears," Hutch says, and Canyon adds, "The worst."

I look into Bentley's eyes, expecting some sort of feeling of pity or connection. There's nothing. He was never my family. There's family you find and family you choose, and life's too short to spend it chasing people who don't treat you the way you deserve.

I step back into the circle of Teddy's arms. The Bad Bear brothers close ranks around us, ready to protect me from anyone or anything.

"Take them to the leech and mindwipe them," Teddy orders. "All of them."

"On it." The Terrible Threes snap into action, hoisting Bentley and the remaining assassins up, leading them off. One of the assassins struggles, and Everest hauls him right off his feet and drags him into the van, like a mother cat carrying a kitten by its scruff.

Matthias appears, looking neat and tidy in pressed jeans and a t-shirt he procured from somewhere. Probably the trunk of his poor car. "Axel's on his way with the Black Wolf pack. I let them know the action's over. And I texted the leech to expect a crowd." Matthias peers at me. "You okay, Lana? I can give you a ride, if you still want to go."

"No," Teddy growls.

"No, I'm good. Much better." My legs are tired. That's a good enough reason to curl into Teddy's chest. "I want to stay with Teddy."

He lifts me into his arms, growling, "I'm not letting you out of my sight."

"All right," Matthias nods. "I can take over from here."

"Good," Teddy hitches me closer. "I need to get my mate home."

15

Lana

The aftermath of adrenaline leaves me drowsy, but I wake up when Teddy kicks open the cabin door. My arms wind around his neck as he carries me like a bride into his cabin.

"Is it safe here?" I look around. It feels like a lifetime since I left this cabin. The place already feels like home.

"It's safe. No more Bentley, no more assassins." Teddy sets me down on the bed and starts tugging off my hiking boots. I flop back on the bed, feeling scraped and bruised but so happy.

Teddy finishes with my boots and traces a scratch on my calf. "Babygirl, I'm so sorry. I fucked up."

I rise up to my elbows. "Just hold me. And never do it again."

"I won't." He climbs onto the bed but hesitates. I'm eager to get to the rip-each-others-clothes-off part of the night, but Teddy looks torn up, so I let him talk. "I wish I could go back in time and erase what I said."

"What's done is done. No more erasing things." I tug

him to lie by my side, where he belongs. "You were freaking out. It's okay. Just tell me you're freaking out next time, and we'll deal with it. Together."

"All right." He takes my hand and kisses my one unscraped knuckle. "Will you forgive me?"

"You're already forgiven."

"I should have never treated you that way."

"You were triggered because of your memories of Tiffany. Darius told me all about it."

"Fucking Darius. I should've told you."

"It's okay. You would've. In the past few days, we've been through a lot. The whole assassin thing... we never got a chance to talk."

"Yeah. There's a lot I need to tell you."

I brace myself, but he cups my face, looking at me with incredible tenderness.

"You're my mate, Lana. That means in all of the universe you're the only one in the world for me. I should have never let you go, Lana, and I never will again. I'm going to be at your side forever."

"Okay," I whisper.

"There's more." He unzips my hoodie. My body goes still, but I'm quivering inside as he tenderly lifts my braids off my shoulders and arranges them around my face.

"Being my mate means we'll be together, forever," he says. "My heart belongs to you, and I'm going to show you what you mean to me." He rests his palm on the side of my neck. "I've talked to my friends, the ones who've mated with humans. There's an instinct shifters have, to mark our mates." He strokes my shoulder lightly with his thumb. "Tonight I want to mark you. I don't want to waste any more time. My bear doesn't want to leave any doubt in your mind that you're mine."

Teddy

Lana blinks up at me through her long lashes. I could spend an eternity looking into her beautiful brown eyes.

"Okay. How does it work?"

"I bite you, and it leaves my scent embedded in your skin, so other shifters know you're mine. It will hurt, but I'll try to be gentle, and the healing will be quicker than an ordinary wound."

"I trust you," she whispers, and it almost brings me to my knees.

"You are perfect for me. I'm going to mark you, but first I'm going to make you feel good."

"As long as you're not too gentle." There's a smile in her voice. She pushes herself up to bring her face close to me. I let our lips collide. I kiss her deeply, letting my tongue dart into her sweet mouth. Probing, plundering. I want her to feel me everywhere.

I kiss down her jaw, along the side of her neck. After tugging off her t-shirt and camisole, I push her onto her back and trail kisses across the swell of her breast.

"My gorgeous, gorgeous female," I murmur.

"Am I?"

"Gorgeous? Hell, yes."

"I meant your female."

"You've been mine since the moment I caught your scent in the woods. I was just too stupid to realize it until it was almost too late." I squeeze her breast and flick my tongue over her dark nipple, teasing it into a stiff point.

"Crazy Viking bear." Her nails score my shoulders through my shirt, so I yank it off, wanting her to mark my skin.

I kiss down her soft belly and unbutton the jean skirt

she made—my talented, creative genius. Once it get it off her, I take her panties off with my teeth then push her knees wide to lick into her.

She cries out the moment my tongue touches her core, lifting her hips to meet my face. I trace inside her lips, parting her soft flesh with my tongue, then spearing her with it. I push back the hood of her clitoris and roll my tongue around the little nubbin until it stiffens and engorges for me. Then I gently pull it between my lips to suck the tiny bud.

"Teddy," she whimpers.

I vow to earn those desperate whimpers at least three times a day until the day we both die. Together, of course. In our sleep. Dreaming about each other.

I take my time, circling her clit, flicking it, sucking it until she squirms and moans and cries out for more. Only then do I rise up, remove my jeans and climb over my beautiful mate.

"I'll be careful," I tell her. I'm warning my bear. We have to be careful with her. She's human. If I bite too deeply or in the wrong place, I could cause real damage.

Lana's beyond caring. She wraps her legs behind my hips and pulls them down to meet hers. I chuckle, lining my cock up with her entrance and rubbing the head in her juices.

She's ready.

More than ready.

I press into her and shudder with the rightness of it. The satisfaction of coupling with my mate—my *acknowledged* mate—is unrivaled.

"Babygirl, you feel so good," I moan, rocking into her with slow, deliberate strokes.

Her head lolls back on the pillow. "You feel good to

me, too, Teddy. I love how big you are. How rough you get."

Aw, fuck. She makes it impossible to hold back. I brace my hands on either side of her head and pick up my speed, slamming home with more force, with more ambition.

I want it to last forever–this claiming of my mate–but there's also the desperate sensation that I will literally die if I don't claim her now.

Right now.

Right fucking…

"Oh fates," I grunt, my balls drawing up tight.

Lana shifts her hips, and I can suddenly dip in even deeper. "Yes!" she cries out. "Teddy, right there!"

I curse, unable to do anything but jackhammer her in the exact spot she requested. I need to satisfy my female. Need to make her come like my life depends on it.

I suppose it does.

"Lana," I choke, feverish now. I sense the change coming on. My fangs lengthening to mark her. My eyes must have changed color, too.

"Oh my God, Teddy. Teddy. Teddy!" Lana screams, and I slam home, both of us coming at the same time. Her tight muscles squeeze my dick, pulsing around my girth as I spend and spend inside her.

I wait to mark her, wait until we've ridden the crest of the orgasm and passed over the other side. I wait until she's gone limp and is moaning softly beneath me. Only then do I lower my head and sink my teeth into the soft flesh of her breast. I bite the upper side, where it rises to meet the shoulder.

She gasps, her eyes flying wide, her hands catching my head.

Oh Fate. I will punch my own face if this was traumatic

for her. I carefully extricate my teeth. "I'm sorry, babygirl. I'm so sorry. Are you okay?" I swipe my tongue across the wounds to clean them and give her the healing properties in my saliva. It's not potent, like a vampire's, but it will help.

"Wow. Um, no, I'm okay. You marked me? You bit my breast."

I stroke my thumb across her soft cheek. "I did, babygirl. I love these breasts. I wanted to see my mark there every time I get you naked."

Her laugh comes out in a rush. "Am I yours now?"

My bear rumbles in satisfaction. *My mate.*

I repeat the words out loud for Lana's benefit. "Forever, babygirl. Bears mate for life. There's no going back now."

"As if I'd ever want to."

The near catastrophe of her mindwipe and assassination are too close for me not to shudder at the idea of losing her. "I will never let you go again. Never, ever," I swear.

"Okay, Viking." Her eyes drift closed, the marking and sex and the insanity of the day catching up with her.

I drop to her side and mold my body around hers, draping an arm under her breasts. "I love you."

"Mmm," she murmurs sleepily. "I love you, too, Viking Bear."

EPILOGUE

Lana

"I'm just saying," I splay my hands to make my case. "His bear is light brown, and he's huge. As big as Everest."

Teddy smiles in the indulgent way he has when I'm being ridiculous and cute. "What are you getting at, babygirl?"

I glance around. Teddy and I are in the middle of the forest, taking the ATV into town. There's no one around, but I take no chances and lower my voice. "Matthias is a pizzly bear."

"Interesting theory. You know, you could just ask him."

"I did! He just looked at me, all mysterious. I got flustered and started talking about the efficacy of human birth control in human-shifter relations. You know, in case your super powerful werebear sperm invades my womb, takes out my IUD and makes me pregnant. I want to be ready."

I can tell Teddy was not expecting this line of conversation. His forehead creases, but he stays remarkably calm. "What did he say?"

"He said twins run in your family." I gulp. As much as I

want a cute little brown bear running around our cabin or our place in LA, I was hoping for a child-free honeymoon. Or three.

"When you get pregnant, whether it's twins or triplets or a combination of both, we'll handle it. Together." Still maneuvering the ATV, he takes my hand and kisses my knuckles, just above my morganite engagement ring.

I let warmth spread through my belly and wait until we've parked to say, "So you want kids with me?'"

"Oh yes. One day." He pulls into the parking lot and leans in. "Until then, I'm going to do my best to fill you with my super shifter sperm at every opportunity. You know, as practice." His teeth nip my ear.

"Mmm." I hum my agreement.

"But first, we gotta get inside for this meeting, or Daisy's going to chew my ear off."

Teddy helps me out of the ATV. I'm in an LA-worthy outfit, a sparkly rose gold jumpsuit with matching high heeled boots. Teddy and I just flew back from my home office for the town meeting. His helicopter business has come in handy. Until I open a GoddessWear office close to Bad Bear mountain, I'm the one and only client. It's not easy flying back and forth for work, but I have a new CEO taking over GoddessWear in a few months, and I'll be able to step back and start planning our wedding. He was reluctant to plan a wedding at all, but I've assured him it'll be intimate—no fuss and no cameras.

I haven't yet told him about the mauve kilts.

"Lana!" Maisy waves as Teddy and I walk into the meeting room. I trot to her and give her a light hug with a double cheek kiss.

"Look at you." I step back to take in her outfit.

"A Lana Langmeyer original." Maisy poses to show off my new creation, the fitted peekaboo dress that's been flying off the shelves. I designed it after Teddy gave me his mark on my breast. When I wear mine, the cutout over my ample cleavage drives him wild.

"The pink suits you," I say.

"It does." Matthias has walked over to our little group. He looks Maisy up and down and nods his approval.

A flush blooms on Maisy's bare chest and spreads up to her face. "T-thank you." She slaps a hand to her now pink neck. "I...uh, gotta go...help my grandma." She rushes off, and I make a mental note to tease Matthias about flirting with the townswomen later.

"Welcome back." Matthias leans in to give me a cheek kiss. "We're up front. We saved you a seat."

At the front of the room, Everest stands like an usher, looming over the row of Bad Bears. The triplets are all slouching. Axel looks like he's asleep. And on the far end, a familiar figure with a blond head and gray suit sits ramrod straight with a briefcase at his feet.

"Is that Darius?" I ask as I settle between Teddy and Matthias.

"Yes," Matthias says. "Here to pitch another real estate project, I believe."

While we're waiting for the meeting to begin, my cell phone beeps, and I pull it out to check the notifications.

"Better put that away," Teddy warns. "Or Daisy—"

"I know, I know." I read the message from my CFO and suppress a squeal.

"Good news?" Teddy asks. He can read me perfectly.

"Great news." I power down my cell and tuck it into my purse. "I'll tell you after."

On stage, Daisy brings the meeting to order. "Everyone, settle down." Maisy hands her a gavel, and she bangs it on the podium. "Today we meet under much different circumstances." She pauses to make sure all eyes are on her. "I'm happy to announce the establishment of the Bad Bear Mountain trust, a non-profit that's dedicated to preserving the beauty and wild spaces on this mountain. As of this morning, the trust has received a ten million dollar donation that we can use to pay off the town's debt." Another pause, but a hush greets Daisy. We're all sitting with our mouths hanging open.

The fake flowers on the mayor's headband bob as she nods. "I'd like to thank the donor, who wishes to remain anonymous. We're still accepting proposals for a new housing development, but in light of the new trust and our debt being eliminated, we can take our time to choose what's best for the mountain. Thank you." She bangs the gavel and, with Maisy's help, wobbles down from the podium, leaving the room a buzz with shock and relief.

"What just happened?" Hutch asks.

"We got very lucky," Matthias murmurs. "Someone with deep pockets must love this mountain very much."

"It's wonderful," I trill, avoiding Matthias' pointed look. He's figured it out. He's always thinking two, three moves ahead. Either that, or his glasses give him X-ray vision. "Shall we go back to the cabin and celebrate?"

As we rise, Darius walks up to us, his hand out like he wants to shake mine. Teddy pulls me into his side, and Darius pockets his hand instead. "Congratulations."

"Why did you say that?" Teddy says.

"You didn't hear? There's a new financial report on GoddessWear. I'll let Lana share the good news."

"Um," I say, in a whisper, even though I know all the werebears around me can hear. "My company just got a billion dollar valuation."

"That's great, babygirl," Teddy murmurs. He has no idea what that means.

"You own the company outright, correct?" Darius asks.

"Yeah."

Teddy blinks. "So that means…"

"I'm a billionaire. Technically. It's not like I have that money in my pocket."

"Fuckin' A," the Terrible Threes say in unison.

"That's great," Matthias says. "Well done."

"Thank you," I whisper.

Teddy waits until we're back in the ATV and rolling through the forest in relative privacy to say, "You were the donor, weren't you?"

"Yeah. Well, technically, the gift came from my parent's estate. Bentley signed off on it and everything." His personality has changed a lot with the mindwipe. Fortunately, for the better. Of course, I'm not sure how his personality could've gotten worse.

Teddy brakes the ATV to a stop and turns to cup my face. "I love you, babygirl."

"I love you, too." My breath caresses his face a second before he claims my mouth in a searing kiss.

A trio of loud whoops make us jolt apart. Hutch, Bern and Canyon come racing out of the forest. Through the trees, the shadows play over the huge forms of both a polar and grizzly–or possibly pizzly–bear.

The Terrible Threes slap the sides of the ATV, hollering and carrying on before they race ahead of us. "C'mon, Lana," Hutch calls. "We'll make a cake!"

Teddy pinches the bridge of his nose.

"I love your family," I tell him.

He sighs and throttles the ATV forward. "I do too. But after cake, I'm kicking them out and tying you to the bed."

"OMG," I whisper.

I can't wait.

Thank you so much for reading Alpha's Rescue! Click here for an exclusive extra scene starring Lana & Teddy called The Not Quite Mile High Club.

If you enjoyed this book, we would so appreciate your review. They make a huge difference for indie authors.

Be sure you've signed up for our newsletters to get word of the next books in the series— up next is Alpha's Command!

Join Renee's Romper Room and Lee Savino's Goddess Group on Facebook to chat about the books and become a part of the Bad Boy Alpha community. Huge hugs—we adore you!

WANT MORE TEDDY & LANA?

Grab The Not Quite Mile High Club here: https://geni.us/Werebearfreebie

WANT MORE SHIFTER OPS?

https://geni.us/Werebearfreebie

WANT FREE BOOKS?

Go to http://subscribepage.com/alphastemp to sign up for Renee Rose's newsletter and receive a free books. In addition to the free stories, you will also get special pricing, exclusive previews and news of new releases.

Download a free Lee Savino book from www.leesavino.com

OTHER TITLES BY RENEE ROSE

Chicago Bratva

"Prelude" in Black Light: Roulette War

The Director

The Fixer

"Owned" in Black Light: Roulette Rematch

The Enforcer

The Soldier

The Hacker

The Bookie

The Cleaner

Vegas Underground Mafia Romance

King of Diamonds

Mafia Daddy

Jack of Spades

Ace of Hearts

Joker's Wild

His Queen of Clubs

Dead Man's Hand

Wild Card

Contemporary
Daddy Rules Series

Fire Daddy

Hollywood Daddy

Stepbrother Daddy

Master Me Series

Her Royal Master

Her Russian Master

Her Marine Master

Yes, Doctor

Double Doms Series

Theirs to Punish

Theirs to Protect

Holiday Feel-Good

Scoring with Santa

Saved

Other Contemporary

Black Light: Valentine Roulette

Black Light: Roulette Redux

Black Light: Celebrity Roulette

Black Light: Roulette War

Black Light: Roulette Rematch

Punishing Portia (written as Darling Adams)

The Professor's Girl

Safe in his Arms

Paranormal

Two Marks Series

Untamed

Tempted

Desired

Enticed

Wolf Ranch Series

Rough

Wild

Feral

Savage

Fierce

Ruthless

Wolf Ridge High Series

Alpha Bully

Alpha Knight

Bad Boy Alphas Series

Alpha's Temptation

Alpha's Danger

Alpha's Prize

Alpha's Challenge

Alpha's Obsession

Alpha's Desire

Alpha's War

Alpha's Mission

Alpha's Bane

Alpha's Secret

Alpha's Prey

Alpha's Sun

Shifter Ops

Alpha's Moon

Alpha's Vow

Alpha's Revenge

Alpha's Fire

Midnight Doms

Alpha's Blood

His Captive Mortal

All Souls Night

Alpha Doms Series

The Alpha's Hunger

The Alpha's Promise

The Alpha's Punishment

The Alpha's Protection (Dirty Daddies)

Other Paranormal

The Winter Storm: An Ever After Chronicle

Sci-Fi

Zandian Masters Series

His Human Slave

His Human Prisoner

Training His Human

His Human Rebel

His Human Vessel
His Mate and Master
Zandian Pet
Their Zandian Mate
His Human Possession

Zandian Brides

Night of the Zandians
Bought by the Zandians
Mastered by the Zandians
Zandian Lights
Kept by the Zandian
Claimed by the Zandian
Stolen by the Zandian

Other Sci-Fi

The Hand of Vengeance
Her Alien Masters

ALSO BY LEE SAVINO

Paranormal romance

The Berserker Saga and Berserker Brides (menage werewolves)

These fierce warriors will stop at nothing to claim their mates.

Draekons (Dragons in Exile) with Lili Zander

(menage alien dragons)

Crashed spaceship. Prison planet. Two big, hulking, bronzed aliens who turn into dragons. The best part? The dragons insist I'm their mate.

Bad Boy Alphas with Renee Rose

(bad boy werewolves)

Never ever date a werewolf.

Tsenturion Masters with Golden Angel

Who knew my e-reader was a portal to another galaxy? Now I'm stuck with a fierce alien commander who wants to claim me as his own.

Planet of Kings with Tabitha Black

My rescuer makes it clear he wants something in return for saving my life...

... an Omega.

Me.

Contemporary Romance

Royal Bad Boy

I'm not falling in love with my arrogant, annoying, sex god boss. Nope. No way.

Royally Fake Fiancé

The Duke of New Arcadia has an image problem only a fiancé can fix. And I'm the lucky lady he's chosen to play Cinderella.

Beauty & The Lumberjacks

After this logging season, I'm giving up sex. For…reasons.

Her Marine Daddy

My hot Marine hero wants me to call him daddy…

Her Dueling Daddies

Two daddies are better than one.

Innocence: dark mafia romance with Stasia Black

I'm the king of the criminal underworld. I always get what I want. And she is my obsession.

Beauty's Beast: a dark romance with Stasia Black

Years ago, Daphne's father stole from me. Now it's time for her to pay her family's debt…with her body.

Wild Whip Ranch with Tristan Rivers

I may give her the discipline she craves, but she'll satisfy my darkest desires.

She'll be my one, my only… my babygirl.

ABOUT RENEE ROSE

USA TODAY BESTSELLING AUTHOR RENEE ROSE loves a dominant, dirty-talking alpha hero! She's sold over a million copies of steamy romance with varying levels of kink. Her books have been featured in USA Today's *Happily Ever After* and *Popsugar*. Named Eroticon USA's Next Top Erotic Author in 2013, she has also won *Spunky and Sassy's* Favorite Sci-Fi and Anthology author, *The Romance Reviews* Best Historical Romance, and has hit the *USA Today* list ten times with her Bad Boy Alphas, Chicago Bratva, and Wolf Ranch series.

Renee loves to connect with readers!
www.reneeroseromance.com
reneeroseauthor@gmail.com

ABOUT LEE SAVINO

Lee Savino is a USA today bestselling author, mom and chocoholic.

Warning: Do not read her Berserker series, or you will be addicted to the huge, dominant warriors who will stop at nothing to claim their mates.

I repeat: Do. Not. Read. The Berserker Saga.

Download a free book from www.leesavino.com (don't read that either. Too much hot, sexy lovin').

20240506184251